THE PELICAN SHAKESPEARE

GENERAL EDITOR ALFRED HARBAGE

THE MERCHANT OF VENICE

WILLIAM SHAKESPEARE

THE MERCHANT OF VENICE

EDITED BY BRENTS STIRLING

PENGUIN BOOKS

Penguin Books Ltd, Harmondsworth,
Middlesex, England
Penguin Books, 40 West 23rd Street,
New York, New York 10010, U.S.A.
Penguin Books Australia Ltd, Ringwood,
Victoria, Australia
Penguin Books Canada Limited, 2801 John Street,
Markham, Ontario, Canada L3R 1B4
Penguin Books (N.Z.) Ltd, 182–190 Wairau Road,
Auckland 10, New Zealand

First published in *The Pelican Shakespeare* 1959
This revised edition first published 1970
Reprinted 1972, 1973, 1975, 1976, 1978, 1980 (twice),
1981, 1982, 1983 (twice), 1984, 1985 (twice), 1986

Library of Congress catalog card number: 78-98354

Printed in the United States of America by
Kingsport Press, Inc., Kingsport, Tennessee
Set in Monotype Ehrhardt

CONTENTS

PUBLISHER'S NOTE

Soon after the thirty-eight volumes forming *The Pelican Shakespeare* had been published, they were brought together in *The Complete Pelican Shakespeare*. The editorial revisions and new textual features are explained in detail in the General Editor's Preface to the one-volume edition. They have all been incorporated in the present volume. The following should be mentioned in particular:

The lines are not numbered in arbitrary units. Instead all lines are numbered which contain a word, phrase, or allusion explained in the glossarial notes. In the occasional instances where there is a long stretch of unannotated text, certain lines are numbered in italics to serve the conventional reference purpose.

The intrusive and often inaccurate place-headings inserted by early editors are omitted (as is becoming standard practise), but for the convenience of those who miss them, an indication of locale now appears as first item in the annotation of each scene.

In the interest of both elegance and utility, each speech-prefix is set in a separate line when the speaker's lines are in verse, except when these words form the second half of a pentameter line. Thus the verse form of the speech is kept visually intact, and turned-over lines are avoided. What is printed as verse and what is printed as prose has, in general, the authority of the original texts. Departures from the original texts in this regard have only the authority of editorial tradition and the judgment of the Pelican editors; and, in a few instances, are admittedly arbitrary.

SHAKESPEARE AND
HIS STAGE

William Shakespeare was christened in Holy Trinity Church, Stratford-upon-Avon, April 26, 1564. His birth is traditionally assigned to April 23. He was the eldest of four boys and two girls who survived infancy in the family of John Shakespeare, glover and trader of Henley Street, and his wife Mary Arden, daughter of a small landowner of Wilmcote. In 1568 John was elected Bailiff (equivalent to Mayor) of Stratford, having already filled the minor municipal offices. The town maintained for the sons of the burgesses a free school, taught by a university graduate and offering preparation in Latin sufficient for university entrance; its early registers are lost, but there can be little doubt that Shakespeare received the formal part of his education in this school.

On November 27, 1582, a license was issued for the marriage of William Shakespeare (aged eighteen) and Ann Hathaway (aged twenty-six), and on May 26, 1583, their child Susanna was christened in Holy Trinity Church. The inference that the marriage was forced upon the youth is natural but not inevitable; betrothal was legally binding at the time, and was sometimes regarded as conferring conjugal rights. Two additional children of the marriage, the twins Hamnet and Judith, were christened on February 2, 1585. Meanwhile the prosperity of the elder Shakespeares had declined, and William was impelled to seek a career outside Stratford.

The tradition that he spent some time as a country

teacher is old but unverifiable. Because of the absence of records his early twenties are called the "lost years," and only one thing about them is certain – that at least some of these years were spent in winning a place in the acting profession. He may have begun as a provincial trouper, but by 1592 he was established in London and prominent enough to be attacked. In a pamphlet of that year, *Groats-worth of Wit*, the ailing Robert Greene complained of the neglect which university writers like himself had suffered from actors, one of whom was daring to set up as a playwright:

... an vpstart Crow, beautified with our feathers, that with his *Tygers hart wrapt in a Players hyde*, supposes he is as well able to bombast out a blanke verse as the best of you: and beeing an absolute *Iohannes fac totum*, is in his owne conceit the onely Shake-scene in a countrey.

The pun on his name, and the parody of his line "O tiger's heart wrapped in a woman's hide" (*3 Henry VI*), pointed clearly to Shakespeare. Some of his admirers protested, and Henry Chettle, the editor of Greene's pamphlet, saw fit to apologize:

... I am as sory as if the originall fault had beene my fault, because my selfe haue seene his demeanor no lesse ciuill than he excelent in the qualitie he professes: Besides, diuers of worship haue reported his vprightnes of dealing, which argues his honesty, and his facetious grace in writting, that approoues his Art. (Prefatory epistle, *Kind-Harts Dreame*)

The plague closed the London theatres for many months in 1592–94, denying the actors their livelihood. To this period belong Shakespeare's two narrative poems, *Venus and Adonis* and *The Rape of Lucrece*, both dedicated to the Earl of Southampton. No doubt the poet was rewarded with a gift of money as usual in such cases, but he did no further dedicating and we have no reliable information on whether Southampton, or anyone else, became his regular patron. His sonnets, first mentioned in 1598 and published without his consent in 1609, are intimate without being

8

explicitly autobiographical. They seem to commemorate the poet's friendship with an idealized youth, rivalry with a more favored poet, and love affair with a dark mistress; and his bitterness when the mistress betrays him in conjunction with the friend; but it is difficult to decide precisely what the "story" is, impossible to decide whether it is fictional or true. The true distinction of the sonnets, at least of those not purely conventional, rests in the universality of the thoughts and moods they express, and in their poignancy and beauty.

In 1594 was formed the theatrical company known until 1603 as the Lord Chamberlain's men, thereafter as the King's men. Its original membership included, besides Shakespeare, the beloved clown Will Kempe and the famous actor Richard Burbage. The company acted in various London theatres and even toured the provinces, but it is chiefly associated in our minds with the Globe Theatre built on the south bank of the Thames in 1599. Shakespeare was an actor and joint owner of this company (and its Globe) through the remainder of his creative years. His plays, written at the average rate of two a year, together with Burbage's acting won it its place of leadership among the London companies.

Individual plays began to appear in print, in editions both honest and piratical, and the publishers became increasingly aware of the value of Shakespeare's name on the title pages. As early as 1598 he was hailed as the leading English dramatist in the *Palladis Tamia* of Francis Meres:

As *Plautus* and *Seneca* are accounted the best for Comedy and Tragedy among the Latines, so *Shakespeare* among the English is the most excellent in both kinds for the stage: for Comedy, witnes his *Gentlemen of Verona*, his *Errors*, his *Loue labors lost*, his *Loue labours wonne* [at one time in print but no longer extant, at least under this title], his *Midsummers night dream*, & his *Merchant of Venice*; for Tragedy, his *Richard the 2*, *Richard the 3*, *Henry the 4*, *King Iohn*, *Titus Andronicus*, and his *Romeo and Iuliet*.

9

The note is valuable both in indicating Shakespeare's prestige and in helping us to establish a chronology. In the second half of his writing career, history plays gave place to the great tragedies; and farces and light comedies gave place to the problem plays and symbolic romances. In 1623, seven years after his death, his former fellow-actors, John Heminge and Henry Condell, cooperated with a group of London printers in bringing out his plays in collected form. The volume is generally known as the First Folio.

Shakespeare had never severed his relations with Stratford. His wife and children may sometimes have shared his London lodgings, but their home was Stratford. His son Hamnet was buried there in 1596, and his daughters Susanna and Judith were married there in 1607 and 1616 respectively. (His father, for whom he had secured a coat of arms and thus the privilege of writing himself gentleman, died in 1601, his mother in 1608.) His considerable earnings in London, as actor-sharer, part owner of the Globe, and playwright, were invested chiefly in Stratford property. In 1597 he purchased for £60 New Place, one of the two most imposing residences in the town. A number of other business transactions, as well as minor episodes in his career, have left documentary records. By 1611 he was in a position to retire, and he seems gradually to have withdrawn from theatrical activity in order to live in Stratford. In March, 1616, he made a will, leaving token bequests to Burbage, Heminge, and Condell, but the bulk of his estate to his family. The most famous feature of the will, the bequest of the second-best bed to his wife, reveals nothing about Shakespeare's marriage; the quaintness of the provision seems commonplace to those familiar with ancient testaments. Shakespeare died April 23, 1616, and was buried in the Stratford church where he had been christened. Within seven years a monument was erected to his memory on the north wall of the chancel. Its portrait bust and the Droeshout engraving on the title page of the First Folio provide the only likenesses with an established claim to authenticity. The best verbal vignette was written by his rival Ben Jonson, the more impressive for being imbedded in a context mainly critical:

. . . I loved the man, and doe honour his memory (on this side idolatry) as much as any. Hee was indeed honest, and of an open and free nature: had an excellent Phantsie, brave notions, and gentle expressions. . . . (*Timber or Discoveries*, ca. 1623–30)

*

The reader of Shakespeare's plays is aided by a general knowledge of the way in which they were staged. The King's men acquired a roofed and artificially lighted theatre only toward the close of Shakespeare's career, and then only for winter use. Nearly all his plays were designed for performance in such structures as the Globe – a three-tiered amphitheatre with a large rectangular platform extending to the center of its yard. The plays were staged by daylight, by large casts brilliantly costumed, but with only a minimum of properties, without scenery, and quite possibly without intermissions. There was a rear stage gallery for action "above," and a curtained rear recess for "discoveries" and other special effects, but by far the major portion of any play was enacted upon the projecting platform, with episode following episode in swift succession, and with shifts of time and place signaled the audience only by the momentary clearing of the stage between the episodes. Information about the identity of the characters and, when necessary, about the time and place of the action was incorporated in the dialogue. No place-headings have been inserted in the present editions; these are apt to obscure the original fluidity of structure, with the emphasis upon action and speech rather than scenic background. (Indications of place are supplied in the foot-notes.) The acting, including that of the youthful apprentices to the profession who performed the parts of women, was highly skillful, with a premium placed upon grace of gesture and beauty of diction. The audiences, a cross section of the general public, commonly numbered a thousand, sometimes more than two thousand. Judged by the type of plays they applauded, these audiences were not only large but also perceptive.

THE TEXTS OF THE PLAYS

About half of Shakespeare's plays appeared in print for the first time in the folio volume of 1623. The others had been published individually, usually in quarto volumes, during his lifetime or in the six years following his death. The copy used by the printers of the quartos varied greatly in merit, sometimes representing Shakespeare's true text, sometimes only a debased version of that text. The copy used by the printers of the folio also varied in merit, but was chosen with care. Since it consisted of the best available manuscripts, or the more acceptable quartos (although frequently in editions other than the first), or of quartos corrected by reference to manuscripts, we have good or reasonably good texts of most of the thirty-seven plays.

In the present series, the plays have been newly edited from quarto or folio texts, depending, when a choice offered, upon which is now regarded by bibliographical specialists as the more authoritative. The ideal has been to reproduce the chosen texts with as few alterations as possible, beyond occasional relineation, expansion of abbreviations, and modernization of punctuation and spelling. Emendation is held to a minimum, and such material as has been added, in the way of stage directions and lines supplied by an alternative text, has been enclosed in square brackets.

None of the plays printed in Shakespeare's lifetime were divided into acts and scenes, and the inference is that the author's own manuscripts were not so divided. In the folio collection, some of the plays remained undivided, some were divided into acts, and some were divided into acts and scenes. During the eighteenth century all of the plays were divided into acts and scenes, and in the Cambridge edition of the mid-nineteenth century, from which the influential Globe text derived, this division was more or less regularized and the lines were numbered. Many useful works of reference employ the act–scene–line apparatus thus established.

Since this act–scene division is obviously convenient, but is of very dubious authority so far as Shakespeare's own structural principles are concerned, or the original manner of staging his plays, a problem is presented to modern editors. In the present series the act–scene division is retained marginally, and may be viewed as a reference aid like the line numbering. A star marks the points of division when these points have been determined by a cleared stage indicating a shift of time and place in the action of the play, or when no harm results from the editorial assumption that there is such a shift. However, at those points where the established division is clearly misleading – that is, where continuous action has been split up into separate "scenes" – the star is omitted and the distortion corrected. This mechanical expedient seemed the best means of combining utility and accuracy.

THE GENERAL EDITOR

INTRODUCTION

The running title of the earliest edition describes *The Merchant of Venice* as a "comicall history" – in terms of the time, a play with a happy ending. The role of Shylock may have been comic also in the sense of being laughable, or even occasionally farcical. Public attitudes of the age suggest this. London playgoers of 1596–97 would have included many who jibed at Dr Roderigo Lopez, the Christianized Portuguese Jew and royal physician, who in 1594 was convicted on doubtful evidence of plotting to poison Queen Elizabeth. As Camden tells the story, just before Lopez was publicly hanged and quartered at Tyburn he protested from the scaffold that "he had loved the Queene as he loved Jesus Christ," an appeal, Camden adds, "which from a man of the Jewish profession was heard not without laughter" (*Annals*, 1635, p. 431). At the time of the Lopez affair Christopher Marlowe's older play, *The Jew of Malta*, was successfully revived by the Admiral's Men, the competitors of Shakespeare's company, and we may suppose that a year or two later *The Merchant* was written and staged. More than a hundred years afterward, in 1701, an adapted version of the play appeared with the comedian Thomas Dogget as Shylock. Of this production Nicholas Rowe, after referring to Shakespeare's Shylock as an "incomparable Character," wrote, " . . . tho' we have seen that Play Receiv'd and Acted as a Comedy and the Part of the *Jew* perform'd by an Excellent Comedian, yet I cannot but think it was design'd

Tragically by the Author" (*Works of Shakespeare*, 1709, I, xix).

Such are a few of the well-known facts about *The Merchant*'s history and the tradition surrounding its earlier production. Facts, however, do not always speak clearly. What these tell us is that our ancestors could find entertainment in Jew-baiting; the question they do not answer is whether Shakespeare catered to that taste fully or with interesting modifications. If the question has an answer, only Shakespeare's play can give it.

Rowe's objection to a comic *Merchant of Venice* is sometimes called the beginning of sentimental interpretation, although he actually asked simply that tragic "fierceness and fellness" replace comedy as the mood and tone of the play. Much more than that ultimately happened. With a succession of eighteenth- and nineteenth-century actors the role of Shylock grew impressively, so that by Irving's day pride of race and noble scorn under persecution had replaced any motives of buffoonery there may have been in earlier tradition. Our own time, frequently one of contradictions, has seen Shylock sometimes cast as a pathetic victim of his environment, and recast in the name of historical accuracy as a comic butt and stock villain. For understandable reasons the historical interpretation has not dominated stage production.

At one extreme, then, is Shylock the scapegoat-clown, and at the other a broken figure who never meant harm with his "merry bond" until "warped" by betrayal and degradation. The reader or playgoer cannot avoid some kind of choice here, but if he respects Shakespeare's art he will see to it, so far as he can, that the play itself guides his judgment. He may, for example, desire a tragic Shylock but decide that the comically romantic fifth act makes this dramatically unworkable.

It is possible, of course, that the play by itself suggests no clear interpretation. One who adopts this view should be sure, however, that he is not transferring his own confusion to Shakespeare. Many critics have said that the Shylock role "ran away" with its creator, and thus remains at variance with the play. They add, correctly, that even with this contradiction *The Merchant* could have been a stage success. But in that case its success would have overlain an artistic failure. Before we assume such a failure, we owe to Shakespeare, and to ourselves, an examination of his play for any design which brings Shylock within a dominant theme and tone of the comedy. Such an inquiry may appear to overemphasize a single character, but its necessary purpose can be a consideration of something larger – the play and its meaning.

Two things at least become clear from Act IV: that Shakespeare's major ethical theme is Christian mercy versus pagan retaliation, and that in thoughtful comedy such moral issues can be the backbone of good entertainment. It is interesting, moreover, that Shakespeare prepares us from the beginning for the trial scene and its disposition of Shylock. Perhaps he realized that if mercy is to win effectively it must triumph over an adversary who is more than the butt of audience ridicule; but in addition he may have sensed that the adversary of mercy must not be allowed undue sympathy or stature, for then his dismissal and the final scene at Belmont would lack dramatic fitness. In any event, Shylock's first scene points to such matters of concern in Shakespeare's working plan. In I, iii, the pattern seems fully formed with a Shylock who is half impressive, half grotesque. Vividly introduced is his habit of phrasal repetition – "three thousand ducats," "three months," echoed and reechoed through the scene. He alternately grovels ("Ho no, no, no . . .") and stiffens ("I will be assured I may . . ."). His variety begins to be interesting; he can leave a formal soliloquy of hate to set forth informally and fondly on the story of Jacob and the lambs which is supposed to justify usury. Insulted for his pains, he briefly submits but then startles us with his first memorable passage of defiance, the "Jewish gaberdine" speech. And he surprises us again with a show of comic abasement and temporizing over the "merry bond."

After being depicted as spoil-sport and miser in his dealings with Jessica and Launcelot, and after being reported by Solanio and Salerio in the "passion so . . . strange, outrageous, and so variable" – "My daughter! O my ducats! O my daughter!" – Shylock encounters the Christians again in Act III. Once more his peculiar repetition, the speech habit one critic describes as "compulsive" : "You knew, none so well, none so well as you . . . ," and later, "Go, Tubal, and meet me at our synagogue ; go, good Tubal ; at our synagogue, Tubal." Once again pathos and farce are combined, as laments for a lost daughter mingle with wails over lost money and treasure exchanged for monkeys. Within this odd complex the finest of Shylock's moments is now reached as Salerio, asking what human flesh is good for, brings on "Hath not a Jew eyes. . . ." Some historians tell us that this passage was meant to be as comic as the surrounding material, and their arguments can be persuasive until, perhaps, one re-experiences the quality of the passage, as well as a very different quality in the speech of Shakespearean characters (e.g., Polonius) when they are clearly meant to be rhetorically absurd. Such absurdity is wholly lacking in Shylock's better moments of retaliation and self-justification.

But if "Hath not a Jew eyes" is a splendid speech, it is not, as often read, a cry for tolerance. It expresses Shylock's just resentment and, at the same time, the vindictive fallacy which will undo him. If like Christians, Jews have eyes, are warmed and cooled by the same winter and summer, then like Christians they will exact revenge. "The villainy you teach me I will execute, and it shall go hard but I will better the instruction." The Elizabethan audience could have warmed to Shylock at this point – not "sympathetically" but with interest and a strange pause in the laughter. It knew as well as any audience has known that what Shylock says about Christian vengeance is true in too large a measure. Many of its members could have sensed, however, that Shylock is about to enter, understandably, the trap that awaits anyone, Jew *or* Christian, who reduces himself to the ethical level of his persecutors by meeting evil with evil. Those who did not perceive this could have caught it plainly as the fourth act unfolded, for it is the substance and point of the trial episode. Shylock's self-styled "Christian" course of revenge condemns him as it would condemn any Christian. Even so, there is much in the play and its age which condemns and ridicules him simply because he is a Jew, and we should not try to explain it away. But Shakespeare, like Marlowe before him, makes it very plain that Jews can learn bad habits from the large family of Christian hypocrites. An Elizabethan dramatist could not have gone much further in clear, unsentimental fair dealing without becoming, for his time, a prophetic visionary.

In a single long scene of Act IV the tables are turned. Again, as this time he moves not toward the trap but into it, Shylock insists that he is imitating Christians in all he does. Just as his persecutors cannot abide cats, pigs, or bagpipes, so he cannot abide Antonio. Once more the repetitious beat of phrase ("I'll not answer that" – "Is it answered?" – "Now for your answer" – "Are you answered?") as Shylock for the last time justifies himself to Christians by citing Christian practise as an example: they own slaves; shall he say, "Let them be free"? They will answer that the slaves are theirs, that they bought them, and so does he answer:

> The pound of flesh which I demand of him
> Is dearly bought, is mine, and I will have it.

The point he makes is scarcely noble, but the passion and the eloquence and the scorn of hypocrisy are – for the moment. The old cormorant is having his hour, but it is soon ended. If in tragedy the heavens may seem to collapse, in comedy the roof falls in, as it now does upon Shylock whetting his knife and chortling of Daniel: he is defeated on the bond and becomes a most uncomfortable recipient of mercy at the hands of Christians from whom he thought he had learned how to be legalistic and vengeful. Only Gratiano (in pointed contrast with the others) remains to cry revenge.

> PORTIA What mercy can you render him, Antonio?
> GRATIANO A halter gratis! Nothing else, for God's sake!

Gratiano, however, speaks alone. Shylock escapes with his life, his freedom, and half his wealth, all of which he had forfeited under his dedicated scheme for imitating the much too common behavior of Christians. These Christians – Portia, the Duke, and Antonio – have smothered him with mercy.

Modern readers often object to the mercy on two grounds; they say that Shylock is wrongfully compelled to forsake his religion and they complain that true mercy would "justify" him, since he resorted to evil because of persecution. To the first complaint only history can attempt an answer: our ancestors believed in eternal damnation and many of them considered it mercy to "enforce" Christianity which alone, they thought, could bring salvation. As for the second objection, Shakespeare is perhaps more clearheaded and less sentimental than many of us. He seems to understand that false Christians have made Shylock what he is; at least he allows Shylock to say so, strenuously and effectively. Yet Shakespeare dramatizes the homely but evasive truth that no matter how "understandable" hate and reprisal are, all who indulge them – even the persecuted – are equally guilty, and only the appearance of mercy can break the chain of evil returned for evil. Hence forgiveness and mercy redeem a discordant world in the fourth act and open the way for concord and a world of music in the fifth.

The Merchant of Venice is much more than Shylock and his bond. Shakespeare's plot skillfully joins several stories: the bond and the pound of flesh, the loyal friendship of Antonio and Bassanio, the suitors and the caskets, the Gratiano–Nerissa and Lorenzo–Jessica courtships, and the episode of the rings. *Il Pecorone* of Ser Giovanni Fiorentino, published at Milan in 1558, contained the pound-of-flesh story (complete with Jewish usurer and lady-as-lawyer), a wooing by "test" (although not the casket device), and the ring story. Marlowe's *The Jew of Malta* may have suggested the Shylock–Jessica relationship. The casket device was available in translation from the *Gesta Romanorum*. Possible minor sources are the ballad of *Gernutus* and Anthony Munday's *Zelauto* (1580). When one reads Shakespeare's sources it becomes clear, however, that the combination of diverse materials in the narrative originals gave him no real help in constructing his play. Those interested in the art of playwriting will enjoy following Shakespeare as he introduces and develops the various elements of *The Merchant* by an adroit sequence of scenes within the fluid Elizabethan staging, which this edition emphasizes. The process culminates in the scene of Bassanio's successful choice, where, as R. G. Moulton observed long ago, the several stories meet: Bassanio chooses, wins, and opens the way for Gratiano; Lorenzo and Jessica, newly eloped, bring in Salerio from Venice to reveal forfeiture of the bond, which raises the claims of friendship; and the lovers exchange the rings which will give such liveliness to the fifth act. An earlier play now lost may have contained some of the plot combinations, but if so, what we know of playwriting before Shakespeare makes it impossible to believe that it could have anticipated his structural plan.

The verse is Shakespeare at his early lyrical best, but its exuberance is controlled by dramatic purpose and fitness. Salerio's opening virtuosity ending in his image of the "wealthy Andrew docked in sand," and Gratiano's lines on men whose faces do "cream and mantle like a standing pond," nicely fit the speakers and the situation. So do Shylock's passages of self-justification in I, iii and III, i. Not only are they expertly set going but they are enhanced by dramatic context. "Hath not a Jew eyes" gains greatly from Salerio's taunting "What's that good for?" which launches it, and from Shylock's lines with Tubal which follow it and qualify its effect. Even the set pieces, the lyrical passages of Act V, are dramatically paced. At this relatively early date Shakespeare had mastered the art of poetry within the exacting medium of drama.

A unifying element of the verse is phrasal repetition in varying forms for varying purposes. As a rhythmic quality of Shylock's speech it runs steadily for four acts, but this important effect, already noted, has its counterparts. Begin, for example, with Shylock's words: "Two thousand ducats in that, and other precious, precious jewels. I would my daughter were dead at my foot, and the jewels in her ear! Would she were hearsed at my foot, and the ducats in her coffin!" (III, i, 77–80) Compare this echoing of phrase with Portia's:

> Though for myself alone
> I would not be ambitious in my wish
> To wish myself much better, yet for you
> I would be trebled twenty times myself,
> A thousand times more fair, ten thousand times more rich,
> That only to stand high in your account,
> I might in virtues, beauties, livings, friends,
> Exceed account.   (III, ii, 150–57)

Add another instance, Bassanio's speech at III, ii, 252–63, and observe finally how the unity in variety extends to the quite different but still analogous passages of V, i, 1–24 ("in such a night") and 192–208 ("the ring").

The Merchant of Venice fully represents Shakespeare's ability to generate "belief" in the fabulous. From the sparse account of one source he drew the wooing test and staged it as the cumulative fantasy of Morocco, Arragon, and Bassanio in their choosing of the caskets. Out of the simple double locale of his source material he built not just two cities, Venice and Belmont, but two symbolic worlds: one commercial, precarious, discordant; the other hospitable, gentle, filled with music. And starting with mere names and events he retold the ancient tale of the usurer and his pound of flesh; the result is Shylock, who in spite of his origin as a stock character is now one of the truly mythic figures of our literature. But these achievements can be misinterpreted. It may seem surprising that a romantic and fanciful play has excited so much moral judgment of its characters (as though they were real people), and so much argument about its law courts, its financial backgrounds, its Jews and its Gentiles (as though they were intendedly historical). In a broad, flexible sense, of course, even romantic fable is historically revealing; Shakespeare's usury theme, for instance, reflects actual economic problems of his time, and Bassanio's advantageous marriage suggests contemporary social customs. The difficulty, however, is that an interesting and frequently subtle relationship between romance and life is sometimes confused with a one-to-one correspondence between the details of fiction and the details of actuality. The literature-and-life relationship is thus mistaken for a kind of identity, and one reason for this is that the artist makes illusion more significant, and therefore more "real," than day-to-day experience. The more imaginatively meaningful he is, the more literally he may be taken. Those who confuse dramatic characters with real people are likely, for example, to consider Bassanio a materialist and opportunist; those who see that art creates its own world with its own emphasis will take him for what he is meant to be – a symbolic quester for love and the Golden Fleece who has the wit to find them in the leaden casket.

University of Washington   BRENTS STIRLING

NOTE ON THE TEXT

The Merchant of Venice was first published in 1600, in a good text which may have been printed from Shakespeare's own draft. From this (the "Heyes" quarto) were printed the "Roberts" quarto of 1619 (falsely dated 1600) and the folio text of 1623, the latter adding a few stage directions possibly derived from a prompt-copy. The present edition closely follows the text of the first quarto. As in other modern editions, the character-name "Salarino," which occurs in the quarto stage directions of I, i; II, iv, vi, viii; III, i, has been eliminated in favor of consistent use of the character-name "Salerio," which occurs elsewhere in the stage directions and in the speeches of the play. The quarto texts are not divided into acts and scenes; the folio text is divided only into acts. The act–scene division supplied marginally for reference in the present edition follows the act division of the folio and adds the subdivision into scenes provided by later editors. All substantive departures from the quarto text other than those noted above are here listed, with the adopted reading in italics followed by the quarto reading in roman. Many of the adopted readings are from the second quarto and the folio.

I, i, 27 *docked* docks   113 *Is that* It is that
II, i, s.d. *Morocco* Morochus   31 *thee,* the   35 *rogue* rage
II, ii, 3–8 *Gobbo* Iobbe
II, iii, 11 *did* do
II, vii, 69 *tombs* timber
II, viii, 39 *Slubber* Slumber
III, i, 95 *Heard* Heere
III, ii, 67 *eyes* eye   81 *vice* voyce   117 *whether* whither
III, iii s.d. *Solanio* Salerio
III, iv, 49 *Padua* Mantua   50 *cousin's* cosin   53 *traject* Tranect
III, v, 20 *e'en* in   70 *merit it* mean it, it   77 *a wife* wife
IV, i, 30 *his state* this states   31 *flint* flints   51 *Master* Maisters
   74 *bleat* bleake   75 *pines* of Pines   100 *is* as   208 *thrice* twice
   396 *Gratiano* Shylock
V, i, 41–42 *Master Lorenzo? Master Lorenzo!* M. Lorenzo, & M. Lorenzo   49 *Sweet soul* (appended to preceding speech)
   152 *give it you* give you

THE MERCHANT
OF VENICE

The Duke of Venice
The Prince of Morocco } *suitors to Portia*
The Prince of Arragon
Antonio, a merchant of Venice
Bassanio, his friend, suitor to Portia
Gratiano
Salerio } *friends to Antonio and Bassanio*
Solanio
Lorenzo, in love with Jessica
Shylock, a Jew
Tubal, a Jew, his friend
Launcelot Gobbo, a clown, servant to Shylock
Old Gobbo, father to Launcelot
Leonardo, servant to Bassanio
Balthasar } *servants to Portia*
Stephano
Portia, an heiress
Nerissa, her gentlewoman-in-waiting
Jessica, daughter to Shylock
Magnificoes of Venice, Court Officers,
    Jailer, Servants, and other Attendants

Scene: *Venice and Belmont*]

THE MERCHANT
OF VENICE

Enter Antonio, Salerio, and Solanio. I, i

ANTONIO

In sooth I know not why I am so sad.
It wearies me, you say it wearies you ;
But how I caught it, found it, or came by it,
What stuff 'tis made of, whereof it is born,
I am to learn ; 5
And such a want-wit sadness makes of me 6
That I have much ado to know myself.

SALERIO

Your mind is tossing on the ocean,
There where your argosies with portly sail – 9
Like signiors and rich burghers on the flood,
Or as it were, the pageants of the sea – 11
Do overpeer the petty traffickers 12
That cursy to them, do them reverence, 13
As they fly by them with their woven wings.

SOLANIO

Believe me, sir, had I such venture forth,
The better part of my affections would
Be with my hopes abroad. I should be still
Plucking the grass to know where sits the wind,
Peering in maps for ports and piers and roads ; 19

I, i A street in Venice **5** *am to learn* have yet to learn **6** *want-wit* fool,
dullard **9** *argosies* large merchant ships; *portly* i.e. swelling, billowing
11 *pageants* i.e. like 'floats' in a procession **12** *overpeer* tower above
13 *cursy* bow **19** *roads* anchorages

And every object that might make me fear
Misfortune to my ventures, out of doubt
Would make me sad.

SALERIO   My wind cooling my broth

23   Would blow me to an ague when I thought
What harm a wind too great might do at sea.
I should not see the sandy hourglass run
But I should think of shallows and of flats,

27   And see my wealthy Andrew docked in sand,
28   Vailing her high top lower than her ribs
To kiss her burial. Should I go to church
And see the holy edifice of stone
And not bethink me straight of dangerous rocks,
Which touching but my gentle vessel's side
Would scatter all her spices on the stream,
Enrobe the roaring waters with my silks –
And in a word, but even now worth this,
And now worth nothing ? Shall I have the thought
To think on this, and shall I lack the thought

38   That such a thing bechanced would make me sad ?
But tell not me ! I know Antonio
Is sad to think upon his merchandise.

ANTONIO
Believe me, no. I thank my fortune for it

42   My ventures are not in one bottom trusted,
43   Nor to one place ; nor is my whole estate
Upon the fortune of this present year.
Therefore my merchandise makes me not sad.

SOLANIO
Why then you are in love.

ANTONIO   Fie, fie !

SOLANIO
Not in love neither ? Then let us say you are sad

---

23 *ague* fit of trembling   **27** *Andrew* name of a ship   **28** *Vailing* bowing
38 *bechanced* having happened   **42** *bottom* ship   **43–44** *nor is . . . year* nor
is all my wealth risked at this one time

Because you are not merry; and 'twere as easy
For you to laugh and leap, and say you are merry
Because you are not sad. Now by two-headed Janus,   50
Nature hath framed strange fellows in her time:
Some that will evermore peep through their eyes
And laugh like parrots at a bagpiper,
And other of such vinegar aspect
That they'll not show their teeth in way of smile
Though Nestor swear the jest be laughable.   56

     Enter Bassanio, Lorenzo, and Gratiano.

Here comes Bassanio your most noble kinsman,
Gratiano, and Lorenzo. Fare ye well;
We leave you now with better company.

SALERIO

I would have stayed till I had made you merry,
If worthier friends had not prevented me.

ANTONIO

Your worth is very dear in my regard.
I take it your own business calls on you,
And you embrace th' occasion to depart.

SALERIO

Good morrow, my good lords.

BASSANIO

Good signiors both, when shall we laugh? Say, when?
You grow exceeding strange. Must it be so?   67

SALERIO

We'll make our leisures to attend on yours.   68
          Exeunt Salerio and Solanio.

LORENZO

My Lord Bassanio, since you have found Antonio,
We two will leave you; but at dinner time
I pray you have in mind where we must meet.

BASSANIO

I will not fail you.

50 *Janus* Roman god with two faces, one smiling and the other sad   56
Nestor old and solemn character in the *Iliad*   67 *strange* like strangers
68 *attend on* wait on, i.e. fit

GRATIANO
You look not well, Signior Antonio.
74   You have too much respect upon the world;
They lose it that do buy it with much care.
Believe me, you are marvellously changed.

ANTONIO
I hold the world but as the world, Gratiano –
A stage where every man must play a part,
And mine a sad one.

GRATIANO   Let me play the fool!
With mirth and laughter let old wrinkles come,
81   And let my liver rather heat with wine
82   Than my heart cool with mortifying groans.
Why should a man whose blood is warm within
84   Sit like his grandsire cut in alabaster?
85   Sleep when he wakes? and creep into the jaundice
By being peevish? I tell thee what, Antonio,
I love thee, and 'tis my love that speaks:
There are a sort of men whose visages
89   Do cream and mantle like a standing pond,
90   And do a willful stillness entertain
91   With purpose to be dressed in an opinion
92   Of wisdom, gravity, profound conceit –
As who should say, 'I am Sir Oracle,
And when I ope my lips, let no dog bark!'
O my Antonio, I do know of these
That therefore only are reputed wise
For saying nothing, when I am very sure
98   If they should speak would almost damn those ears,
Which hearing them would call their brothers fools.
I'll tell thee more of this another time.

74 *respect upon* concern for   81 *liver* (to Elizabethans, the seat of the emotions)   82 *mortifying* deadening, destructive of life and joy   84 *alabaster* stone used for monuments   85 *jaundice* condition of biliousness, depression   89 *cream and mantle* i.e. become dull (with scum)   90 *entertain* take on, assume   91 *opinion* reputation (so also in l. 102)   92 *conceit* thought   98–99 *If they . . . fools* (see Matthew v, 22: '. . . but whosoever shall say, Thou fool, shall be in danger of hell fire.')

But fish not with this melancholy bait
For this fool gudgeon, this opinion.   102
Come, good Lorenzo. Fare ye well awhile ;
I'll end my exhortation after dinner.

LORENZO
Well, we will leave you then till dinner time.
I must be one of these same dumb wise men,
For Gratiano never lets me speak.

GRATIANO
Well, keep me company but two years moe,   108
Thou shalt not know the sound of thine own tongue.

ANTONIO
Fare you well ; I'll grow a talker for this gear.   110

GRATIANO
Thanks i' faith ; for silence is only commendable
In a neat's tongue dried and a maid not vendible.   112

Exeunt [Gratiano and Lorenzo].

ANTONIO Is that anything now ?

BASSANIO Gratiano speaks an infinite deal of nothing,
more than any man in all Venice. His reasons are as two
grains of wheat hid in two bushels of chaff : you shall
seek all day ere you find them, and when you have them
they are not worth the search.

ANTONIO
Well, tell me now what lady is the same
To whom you swore a secret pilgrimage,
That you to-day promised to tell me of.

BASSANIO
'Tis not unknown to you, Antonio,
How much I have disabled mine estate   123
By something showing a more swelling port   124
Than my faint means would grant continuance.   125

---

102 *gudgeon* a fish   108 *moe* more   110 *for this gear* because of this 'stuff'
(what you have just said)   112 *neat's* ox's ; *vendible* marketable, i.e. mar-
riageable   123 *disabled* impaired, reduced   124 *something . . . port* some-
what exhibiting a more lavish behavior   125 *grant continuance* allow to
continue

126   Nor do I now make moan to be abridged
127   From such a noble rate ; but my chief care
    Is to come fairly off from the great debts
    Wherein my time, something too prodigal,
130   Hath left me gaged. To you, Antonio,
    I owe the most in money and in love,
    And from your love I have a warranty
    To unburden all my plots and purposes
    How to get clear of all the debts I owe.

ANTONIO

    I pray you, good Bassanio, let me know it,
    And if it stand as you yourself still do,
    Within the eye of honor, be assured
    My purse, my person, my extremest means
    Lie all unlocked to your occasions.

BASSANIO

140   In my schooldays, when I had lost one shaft
141   I shot his fellow of the selfsame flight
    The selfsame way, with more advisèd watch,
    To find the other forth ; and by adventuring both
    I oft found both. I urge this childhood proof
145   Because what follows is pure innocence.
    I owe you much, and like a willful youth
    That which I owe is lost ; but if you please
    To shoot another arrow that self way
    Which you did shoot the first, I do not doubt,
150   As I will watch the aim, or to find both
    Or bring your latter hazard back again
    And thankfully rest debtor for the first.

ANTONIO

153   You know me well, and herein spend but time

---

126 *abridged* cut down, reduced   127 *noble rate* high scale   130 *gaged*
pledged for, owing   140 *shaft* arrow   141 *selfsame flight* same size and kind
145 *innocence* childlike sincerity, with perhaps a touch of folly   150 *or*
either   153–54 *spend . . . circumstance* i.e. needlessly persuade me with
elaborate talk

To wind about my love with circumstance;
And out of doubt you do me now more wrong
In making question of my uttermost   156
Than if you had made waste of all I have.
Then do but say to me what I should do
That in your knowledge may by me be done,
And I am prest unto it. Therefore speak.   160

BASSANIO
In Belmont is a lady richly left;   161
And she is fair, and fairer than that word,
Of wondrous virtues. Sometimes from her eyes
I did receive fair speechless messages.
Her name is Portia, nothing undervalued   165
To Cato's daughter, Brutus' Portia;
Nor is the wide world ignorant of her worth,
For the four winds blow in from every coast
Renownèd suitors, and her sunny locks
Hang on her temples like a golden fleece,   170
Which makes her seat of Belmont Colchos' strond,   171
And many Jasons come in quest of her.
O my Antonio, had I but the means
To hold a rival place with one of them,
I have a mind presages me such thrift   175
That I should questionless be fortunate!

ANTONIO
Thou know'st that all my fortunes are at sea;
Neither have I money, nor commodity   178
To raise a present sum. Therefore go forth.
Try what my credit can in Venice do;
That shall be racked even to the uttermost   181
To furnish thee to Belmont, to fair Portia.

---

156 *making . . . uttermost* questioning that I will do all I can   **160** *prest unto* ready for   **161** *richly left* rich by inheritance   **165–66** *nothing undervalued To* of no less worth than   **170–72** *golden . . . of her* (reference to Jason's mythical quest for the Golden Fleece)   **171** *strond* shore   **175** *thrift* profit, thriving   **178** *commodity* goods (?), business connection (?)   **181** *racked* stretched, as on the rack

Go presently inquire, and so will I,
Where money is; and I no question make
85   To have it of my trust or for my sake.   *Exeunt.*

*

I, ii   *Enter Portia with her waiting woman, Nerissa.*

1 PORTIA By my troth, Nerissa, my little body is aweary of
this great world.

NERISSA You would be, sweet madam, if your miseries
were in the same abundance as your good fortunes are;
and yet for aught I see, they are as sick that surfeit with
too much as they that starve with nothing. It is no mean

7   happiness, therefore, to be seated in the mean; super-
8   fluity comes sooner by white hairs, but competency
lives longer.

10 PORTIA Good sentences, and well pronounced.

NERISSA They would be better if well followed.

PORTIA If to do were as easy as to know what were good
to do, chapels had been churches, and poor men's cot-
14   tages princes' palaces. It is a good divine that follows his
own instructions; I can easier teach twenty what were
good to be done than to be one of the twenty to follow
mine own teaching. The brain may devise laws for the
18   blood, but a hot temper leaps o'er a cold decree; such a
19   hare is madness the youth to skip o'er the meshes of good
20   counsel the cripple. But this reasoning is not in the fashion to choose me a husband. O me, the word 'choose'! I
may neither choose who I would nor refuse who I dis-
23   like, so is the will of a living daughter curbed by the will

---

185 *of my trust . . . sake* on the basis of my credit or as a personal favor
I, ii The house of Portia in Belmont   1 *troth* faith   7 *seated . . . mean*
with neither too much nor too little   8 *comes sooner by* gets sooner; *competency* modest means   10 *sentences* maxims, proverbs   14 *divine* preacher
18 *temper* temperament   19 *meshes* net for catching hares   19–20 *good
counsel* wisdom   20 *not . . . fashion* not the way   23–24 *will of a dead father*
dead father's bequest (with pun)

of a dead father. Is it not hard, Nerissa, that I cannot
choose one, nor refuse none? 25

NERISSA Your father was ever virtuous, and holy men at
their death have good inspirations. Therefore the lott'ry
that he hath devised in these three chests of gold, silver,
and lead – whereof who chooses his meaning chooses
you – will no doubt never be chosen by any rightly but
one who you shall rightly love. But what warmth is
there in your affection towards any of these princely
suitors that are already come?

PORTIA I pray thee overname them; and as thou namest 34
them I will describe them, and according to my description level at my affection. 36

NERISSA First, there is the Neapolitan prince.

PORTIA Ay, that's a colt indeed, for he doth nothing but
talk of his horse, and he makes it a great appropriation 39
to his own good parts that he can shoe him himself. I am 40
much afeard my lady his mother played false with a smith.

NERISSA Then is there the County Palatine. 42

PORTIA He doth nothing but frown – as who should say,
'An you will not have me, choose!' He hears merry tales 44
and smiles not; I fear he will prove the weeping philosopher when he grows old, being so full of unmannerly
sadness in his youth. I had rather be married to a
death's-head with a bone in his mouth than to either of
these. God defend me from these two!

NERISSA How say you by the French lord, Monsieur Le
Bon?

PORTIA God made him, and therefore let him pass for a
man. In truth, I know it is a sin to be a mocker, but he –
why he hath a horse better than the Neapolitan's, a better bad habit of frowning than the Count Palatine; he is

---

25 *refuse none* refuse any a chance at the *lott'ry* (l. 27)   34 *overname them* 'go
over' their names   36 *level . . . affection* try to decide, or to guess, how I feel
toward them   39 *appropriation* addition   40 *parts* abilities   42 *County*
count   44 *An* if; *choose* choose whom you please (?), I defy you to choose
anyone else (?)

56 every man in no man. If a throstle sing, he falls straight
a-cap'ring; he will fence with his own shadow. If I
should marry him, I should marry twenty husbands. If
he would despise me, I would forgive him; for if he
love me to madness, I shall never requite him.

NERISSA What say you then to Falconbridge, the young
baron of England?

PORTIA You know I say nothing to him, for he under-
stands not me, nor I him. He hath neither Latin, French,
nor Italian; and you will come into the court and swear
that I have a poor pennyworth in the English. He is a
67 proper man's picture, but alas! who can converse with a
68 dumb-show? How oddly he is suited! I think he bought
69 his doublet in Italy, his round hose in France, his
bonnet in Germany, and his behavior everywhere.

NERISSA What think you of the Scottish lord, his neighbor?

PORTIA That he hath a neighborly charity in him, for he
borrowed a box of the ear of the Englishman and swore
he would pay him again when he was able. I think the
75 Frenchman became his surety and sealed under for
another.

NERISSA How like you the young German, the Duke of
Saxony's nephew?

PORTIA Very vilely in the morning when he is sober, and
most vilely in the afternoon when he is drunk. When
he is best he is a little worse than a man, and when he is
worst he is little better than a beast. An the worst fall
83 that ever fell, I hope I shall make shift to go without him.

NERISSA If he should offer to choose, and choose the
right casket, you should refuse to perform your father's
will if you should refuse to accept him.

PORTIA Therefore, for fear of the worst, I pray thee set a

---

56 *throstle* thrush **67** *proper* handsome **68** *dumb-show* pantomime;
suited dressed **69** *doublet* coat; *hose* breeches **75** *became his surety*
(reference to the alliance of France and Scotland against England); *sealed
under* put his seal under the Scot's **83** *make shift* manage

deep glass of Rhenish wine on the contrary casket, for if 88
the devil be within and that temptation without, I know
he will choose it. I will do anything, Nerissa, ere I will
be married to a sponge.

NERISSA You need not fear, lady, the having any of these
lords. They have acquainted me with their determina-
tions, which is indeed to return to their home and to
trouble you with no more suit, unless you may be won
by some other sort than your father's imposition, de- 96
pending on the caskets.

PORTIA If I live to be as old as Sibylla, I will die as chaste 98
as Diana unless I be obtained by the manner of my
father's will. I am glad this parcel of wooers are so
reasonable, for there is not one among them but I dote
on his very absence; and I pray God grant them a fair
departure.

NERISSA Do you not remember, lady, in your father's
time, a Venetian, a scholar and a soldier, that came
hither in company of the Marquis of Montferrat?

PORTIA Yes, yes, it was Bassanio – as I think, so was he
called.

NERISSA True, madam. He, of all the men that ever my
foolish eyes looked upon, was the best deserving a fair
lady.   110

PORTIA I remember him well, and I remember him
worthy of thy praise.
      Enter a Servingman.
How now? What news?

SERVINGMAN The four strangers seek for you, madam,
to take their leave; and there is a forerunner come from
a fifth, the Prince of Morocco, who brings word the
Prince his master will be here to-night.

PORTIA If I could bid the fifth welcome with so good

---

88 *contrary* other, or 'wrong'   96 *sort* way   98 *Sibylla* prophetess to whom
Apollo promised as many years of life as there were grains in her handful of
sand

heart as I can bid the other four farewell, I should be
120 glad of his approach. If he have the condition of a saint
121 and the complexion of a devil, I had rather he should
122 shrive me than wive me. Come, Nerissa. Sirrah, go
before. Whiles we shut the gate upon one wooer, another knocks at the door.   *Exeunt.*

*

I, iii   *Enter Bassanio with Shylock the Jew.*

SHYLOCK Three thousand ducats – well.

BASSANIO Ay, sir, for three months.

SHYLOCK For three months – well.

BASSANIO For the which, as I told you, Antonio shall be
5   bound.

SHYLOCK Antonio shall become bound – well.

7 BASSANIO May you stead me? Will you pleasure me?
Shall I know your answer?

SHYLOCK Three thousand ducats for three months, and
Antonio bound.

BASSANIO Your answer to that.

12 SHYLOCK Antonio is a good man.

BASSANIO Have you heard any imputation to the contrary?

SHYLOCK Ho no, no, no, no! My meaning in saying he is a
15   good man is to have you understand me that he is suffi-
16   cient. Yet his means are in supposition. He hath an
argosy bound to Tripolis, another to the Indies; I
18   understand, moreover, upon the Rialto, he hath a third

---

120 *condition* character, nature   **121** *complexion . . . devil* (refers to Morocco's blackness which was also the devil's color)   **122–24** *shrive . . . door* (note
the rhymes within the prose)   **122** *shrive me* hear my confession; *Sirrah*
form of address to servants
I, iii A public place in Venice   **5** *bound* responsible, as a surety   **7** *stead*
accommodate   **12** *good* reliable in business dealings   **15** *sufficient* solvent
16 *in supposition* uncertain   **18** *Rialto* Venetian Merchants' Exchange

at Mexico, a fourth for England – and other ventures he
hath squand'red abroad. But ships are but boards,
sailors but men; there be land rats and water rats,
water thieves and land thieves – I mean pirates; and   22
then there is the peril of waters, winds, and rocks. The
man is, notwithstanding, sufficient. Three thousand
ducats – I think I may take his bond.

BASSANIO Be assured you may.

SHYLOCK I will be assured I may; and that I may be
assured, I will bethink me. May I speak with Antonio?

BASSANIO If it please you to dine with us.

SHYLOCK Yes, to smell pork, to eat of the habitation
which your prophet the Nazarite conjured the devil into!   31
I will buy with you, sell with you, talk with you, walk
with you, and so following; but I will not eat with you,
drink with you, nor pray with you. What news on the
Rialto? Who is he comes here?

    Enter Antonio.

BASSANIO
This is Signior Antonio.

SHYLOCK *[aside]*
How like a fawning publican he looks.   37
I hate him for he is a Christian;   38
But more, for that in low simplicity
He lends out money gratis and brings down
The rate of usance here with us in Venice.   41
If I can catch him once upon the hip,   42
I will feed fat the ancient grudge I bear him.
He hates our sacred nation, and he rails,
Even there where merchants most do congregate,
On me, my bargains, and my well-won thrift,

22 *pirates* pi-rats (?)   31 *Nazarite . . . into* (reference to Christ's casting of
evil spirits into a herd of swine; see Luke viii, 26–33, Mark v, 1–13)   37
publican innkeeper   38 *for* because   41 *usance* interest   42 *catch . . . hip*
(figure of speech from wrestling)

Which he calls interest. Cursèd be my tribe
If I forgive him.

BASSANIO   Shylock, do you hear?

SHYLOCK

49   I am debating of my present store,
And by the near guess of my memory

51   I cannot instantly raise up the gross
Of full three thousand ducats. What of that?
Tubal, a wealthy Hebrew of my tribe,
Will furnish me. But soft, how many months
Do you desire? *[to Antonio]* Rest you fair, good signior!
Your worship was the last man in our mouths.

ANTONIO

Shylock, albeit I neither lend nor borrow

58   By taking nor by giving of excess,

59   Yet to supply the ripe wants of my friend,

60   I'll break a custom. *[to Bassanio]* Is he yet possessed
How much ye would?

SHYLOCK   Ay, ay, three thousand ducats.

ANTONIO

And for three months.

SHYLOCK

I had forgot – three months, you told me so.
Well then, your bond. And let me see – but hear you,

65   Methoughts you said you neither lend nor borrow
Upon advantage.

ANTONIO   I do never use it.

SHYLOCK

67   When Jacob grazed his uncle Laban's sheep –
This Jacob from our holy Abram was,
As his wise mother wrought in his behalf,
The third possessor; ay, he was the third –

ANTONIO

And what of him? Did he take interest?

---

49 *store* wealth   51 *gross* full amount   58 *excess* interest   59 *ripe* immediate   60–61 *possessed . . . would* informed of how much you want   65 *Methoughts* it seemed to me   67 *Jacob* (see Genesis xxvii, xxx, 25–43)

Read The Way.

SHYLOCK

No, not take interest – not as you would say
Directly int'rest. Mark what Jacob did:
When Laban and himself were compromised   74
That all the eanlings which were streaked and pied   75
Should fall as Jacob's hire, the ewes being rank *in heat*   76
In end of autumn turnèd to the rams;
And when the work of generation was
Between these woolly breeders in the act,
The skillful shepherd peeled me certain wands,   80
And in the doing of the deed of kind   81
He stuck them up before the fulsome ewes,
Who then conceiving, did in eaning time   83
Fall parti-colored lambs, and those were Jacob's.
This was a way to thrive, and he was blest;
And thrift is blessing if men steal it not.

ANTONIO

This was a venture, sir, that Jacob served for,   87
A thing not in his power to bring to pass,
But swayed and fashioned by the hand of heaven.
Was this inserted to make interest good?   90
Or is your gold and silver ewes and rams?

SHYLOCK

I cannot tell; I make it breed as fast.
But note me, signior –
ANTONIO   Mark you this, Bassanio,
The devil can cite Scripture for his purpose.
An evil soul producing holy witness
Is like a villain with a smiling cheek,
A goodly apple rotten at the heart.
O what a goodly outside falsehood hath!

---

74 *compromised* agreed **75** *eanlings* lambs; *pied* spotted **76** *hire* share,
recompense; *rank* in heat **80** *peeled me* peeled (a colloquialism); *wands*
branches, shoots **81** *kind* nature **83** *eaning* lambing **87–88** *venture . . .
pass* i.e. a commercial venture of some uncertainty **90** *inserted . . . good*
brought in to justify charging interest

41

SHYLOCK

Three thousand ducats – 'tis a good round sum.

Three months from twelve – then let me see, the rate –

ANTONIO

101   Well, Shylock, shall we be beholding to you?

SHYLOCK

Signior Antonio, many a time and oft

103   In the Rialto you have rated me

About my moneys and my usances.

Still have I borne it with a patient shrug,

106   For suff'rance is the badge of all our tribe.

You call me misbeliever, cutthroat dog,

108   And spit upon my Jewish gaberdine,

And all for use of that which is mine own.

Well then, it now appears you need my help.

111   Go to then. You come to me and you say,

'Shylock, we would have moneys' – you say so,

113   You that did void your rheum upon my beard

And foot me as you spurn a stranger cur

Over your threshold! Moneys is your suit.

What should I say to you? Should I not say,

'Hath a dog money? is it possible

A cur can lend three thousand ducats?' Or

Shall I bend low, and in a bondman's key,

With bated breath and whisp'ring humbleness,

Say this:

'Fair sir, you spit on me on Wednesday last,

You spurned me such a day, another time

You called me dog; and for these courtesies

I'll lend you thus much moneys'?

ANTONIO

I am as like to call thee so again,

To spit on thee again, to spurn thee too.

---

101 *beholding* in debt   103 *rated* railed at, reviled   106 *suff'rance* patience, endurance   108 *gaberdine* cloak   111 *Go to* (exclamation of impatience, like 'Come, come!')   113 *rheum* spittle, mucous discharge

If thou wilt lend this money, lend it not
As to thy friends – for when did friendship take
A breed for barren metal of his friend ? –   130
But lend it rather to thine enemy,
Who if he break, thou mayst with better face   132
Exact the penalty.

SHYLOCK   Why look you, how you storm !
I would be friends with you and have your love,
Forget the shames that you have stained me with,
Supply your present wants, and take no doit   136
Of usance for my moneys ; and you'll not hear me.
This is kind I offer.   138

BASSANIO
This were kindness.

SHYLOCK   This kindness will I show :
Go with me to a notary ; seal me there
Your single bond, and – in a merry sport –   141
If you repay me not on such a day,
In such a place, such sum or sums as are
Expressed in the condition, let the forfeit
Be nominated for an equal pound   145
Of your fair flesh, to be cut off and taken
In what part of your body pleaseth me.

ANTONIO
Content, in faith. I'll seal to such a bond,
And say there is much kindness in the Jew.

BASSANIO
You shall not seal to such a bond for me !
I'll rather dwell in my necessity.   151

ANTONIO
Why fear not, man ; I will not forfeit it.

---

130 *breed . . . metal* offspring of barren metal, i.e. interest   132 *break* go
bankrupt   136 *doit* coin of very small value   138 *kind I offer* i.e. a kindly
offer (with a suggestion of 'natural' dealing; Antonio has called usury
unnatural)   141 *single* without other security   145 *nominated* named, pre-
scribed; *equal* exact   151 *dwell . . . necessity* i.e. remain in need

Within these two months – that's a month before
This bond expires – I do expect return
Of thrice three times the value of this bond.

SHYLOCK

O father Abram, what these Christians are,
Whose own hard dealings teaches them suspect
The thoughts of others ! Pray you tell me this :
159   If he should break his day, what should I gain
By the exaction of the forfeiture ?
A pound of man's flesh taken from a man
Is not so estimable, profitable neither,
As flesh of muttons, beefs, or goats. I say
To buy his favor I extend this friendship.
If he will take it, so ; if not, adieu.
166   And for my love I pray you wrong me not.

ANTONIO

Yes, Shylock, I will seal unto this bond.

SHYLOCK

Then meet me forthwith at the notary's ;
Give him direction for this merry bond,
170   And I will go and purse the ducats straight,
171   See to my house, left in the fearful guard
Of an unthrifty knave, and presently
I'll be with you.   *Exit.*
173   ANTONIO   Hie thee, gentle Jew.
The Hebrew will turn Christian ; he grows kind.

BASSANIO

I like not fair terms and a villain's mind.

ANTONIO

Come on. In this there can be no dismay ;
My ships come home a month before the day.   *Exeunt.*

*

159 *break his day* fail to pay on the due date   166 *wrong me not* think not
unjustly of me   170 *purse* procure, gather   171 *fearful* precarious   173
gentle (with pun on 'gentile' ?)

[Flourish of cornets.] Enter [the Prince of] Morocco, II, i
a tawny Moor all in white, and three or four Followers
accordingly, with Portia, Nerissa, and their Train.

MOROCCO
Mislike me not for my complexion,
The shadowed livery of the burnished sun,   2
To whom I am a neighbor and near bred.
Bring me the fairest creature northward born,
Where Phoebus' fire scarce thaws the icicles,   5
And let us make incision for your love   6
To prove whose blood is reddest, his or mine.
I tell thee, lady, this aspect of mine   8
Hath feared the valiant. By my love I swear   9
The best-regarded virgins of our clime
Have loved it too. I would not change this hue,
Except to steal your thoughts, my gentle queen.   12

PORTIA
In terms of choice I am not solely led   13
By nice direction of a maiden's eyes.   14
Besides, the lott'ry of my destiny
Bars me the right of voluntary choosing.
But if my father had not scanted me,   17
And hedged me by his wit to yield myself
His wife who wins me by that means I told you,
Yourself, renownèd Prince, then stood as fair
As any comer I have looked on yet
For my affection.

MOROCCO   Even for that I thank you.
Therefore I pray you lead me to the caskets
To try my fortune. By this scimitar,
That slew the Sophy and a Persian prince   25
That won three fields of Sultan Solyman,   26

II, i Within Portia's house in Belmont   2 *shadowed . . . sun* dark dress of
the sun's subjects or retainers, i.e. dark skin   5 *Phoebus'* the sun's   6 *make
incision* cut to draw blood   8 *aspect* countenance   9 *feared* frightened
12 *steal your thoughts* i.e. win your favor   13 *terms* matters   14 *nice* fastidi-
ous   17 *scanted* restricted   25 *Sophy* Shah of Persia   26 *Solyman* a
Turkish ruler

27   I would o'erstare the sternest eyes that look,
      Outbrave the heart most daring on the earth,
      Pluck the young sucking cubs from the she-bear,
30   Yea, mock the lion when 'a roars for prey,
      To win thee, lady. But alas the while,
32   If Hercules and Lichas play at dice
      Which is the better man, the greater throw
      May turn by fortune from the weaker hand.
35   So is Alcides beaten by his rogue,
      And so may I, blind Fortune leading me,
      Miss that which one unworthier may attain,
      And die with grieving.

PORTIA   You must take your chance,
      And either not attempt to choose at all
      Or swear before you choose, if you choose wrong
      Never to speak to lady afterward
42   In way of marriage. Therefore be advised.

MOROCCO
43   Nor will not. Come, bring me unto my chance.

PORTIA
44   First, forward to the temple; after dinner
      Your hazard shall be made.

MOROCCO   Good fortune then,
      To make me blest or cursèd'st among men!

                        [Flourish of cornets.] Exeunt.

                            *

II, ii   *Enter [Launcelot Gobbo,] the Clown, alone.*

LAUNCELOT Certainly my conscience will serve me to
      run from this Jew my master. The fiend is at mine elbow

---

27 *o'erstare* outstare   30 *'a* he   32 *Lichas* servant of Hercules   35 *Alcides*
Hercules; *rogue* menial servant   42 *be advised* take care   43 *Nor will not* i.e.
I agree to the conditions just imposed   44 *to the temple* i.e. to swear the
oath
II, ii A street in Venice

and tempts me, saying to me, 'Gobbo, Launcelot Gobbo, good Launcelot,' or 'good Gobbo,' or 'good Launcelot Gobbo – use your legs, take the start, run away.'
My conscience says, 'No. Take heed, honest Launcelot;
take heed, honest Gobbo,' or as aforesaid, 'honest Launcelot Gobbo – do not run; scorn running with thy heels.' 8
Well, the most courageous fiend bids me pack. 'Fia!' 9
says the fiend; 'away!' says the fiend. 'For the heavens, 10
rouse up a brave mind,' says the fiend, 'and run.' Well,
my conscience hanging about the neck of my heart says
very wisely to me, 'My honest friend Launcelot, being
an honest man's son' – or rather 'an honest woman's
son,' for indeed my father did something smack, some- 15
thing grow to; he had a kind of taste – Well, my conscience says, 'Launcelot, budge not.' 'Budge,' says the
fiend. 'Budge not,' says my conscience. 'Conscience,'
say I, 'you counsel well.' 'Fiend,' say I, 'you counsel
well.' To be ruled by my conscience, I should stay with
the Jew my master who, God bless the mark, is a kind of 21
devil; and to run away from the Jew, I should be ruled
by the fiend who, saving your reverence, is the devil 23
himself. Certainly the Jew is the very devil incarnation; 24
and in my conscience, my conscience is but a kind of
hard conscience to offer to counsel me to stay with the
Jew. The fiend gives the more friendly counsel. I will
run, fiend; my heels are at your commandment; I will
run.

    Enter Old Gobbo with a basket.

GOBBO Master young man, you, I pray you, which is the
    way to Master Jew's?
LAUNCELOT *[aside]* O heavens, this is my true-begotten

---

8 *scorn . . . heels* i.e. scorn running emphatically (by running from it? or
kicking at it?)   9 *pack* be off; *Fia* away (Italian '*via*')   10 *For the heavens*
for heaven's sake   15–16 *did something . . . taste* i.e. was a bit promiscu-
ous (?)   21, 23 *God . . . mark, saving . . . reverence* (conventional phrases
of apology for what one is about to say)   24 *incarnation* incarnate

32   father who, being more than sand-blind, high-gravel-
blind, knows me not. I will try confusions with him.

GOBBO Master young gentleman, I pray you which is the
way to Master Jew's?

LAUNCELOT Turn up on your right hand at the next
turning, but at the next turning of all, on your left;

38   marry, at the very next turning turn of no hand, but
turn down indirectly to the Jew's house.

40 GOBBO Be God's sonties, 'twill be a hard way to hit! Can
you tell me whether one Launcelot that dwells with
him, dwell with him or no?

43 LAUNCELOT Talk you of young Master Launcelot?

44   *[aside]* Mark me now; now will I raise the waters. –
Talk you of young Master Launcelot?

GOBBO No master, sir, but a poor man's son. His father,
though I say't, is an honest exceeding poor man and,

48   God be thanked, well to live.

LAUNCELOT Well, let his father be what 'a will, we talk
of young Master Launcelot.

GOBBO Your worship's friend, and Launcelot, sir.

52 LAUNCELOT But I pray you, ergo old man, ergo I beseech you, talk you of young Master Launcelot?

GOBBO Of Launcelot, an't please your mastership.

LAUNCELOT Ergo, Master Launcelot. Talk not of Master
Launcelot, father, for the young gentleman, according

57   to Fates and Destinies and such odd sayings, the Sisters
Three and such branches of learning, is indeed deceased,
or as you would say in plain terms, gone to heaven.

GOBBO Marry, God forbid! The boy was the very staff of
my age, my very prop.

LAUNCELOT Do I look like a cudgel or a hovel-post, a

---

32 *sand-blind* partly blind   32–33 *high-gravel-blind* blinder than sand-blind
(cf. 'stone-blind')   38 *marry* to be sure (an interjection)   40 *Be* by;
sonties saints (?), sanctities (?)   43 *Master* title applied to young gentlemen
44 *raise the waters* i.e. start something (raise tears?)   48 *well to live* lives
comfortably (?), with prospect of a long life (?)   52 *ergo* therefore   57–58
Sisters Three the three Fates

staff or a prop? Do you know me, father?

GOBBO Alack the day, I know you not, young gentleman! but I pray you tell me, is my boy, God rest his
soul, alive or dead?

LAUNCELOT Do you not know me, father?

GOBBO Alack, sir, I am sand-blind! I know you not.

LAUNCELOT Nay, indeed if you had your eyes you might
fail of the knowing me; it is a wise father that knows his   70
own child. Well, old man, I will tell you news of your
son. [Kneels.] Give me your blessing. Truth will come
to light; murder cannot be hid long – a man's son may,
but in the end truth will out.

GOBBO Pray you, sir, stand up. I am sure you are not
Launcelot my boy.

LAUNCELOT Pray you let's have no more fooling about it,
but give me your blessing. I am Launcelot – your boy
that was, your son that is, your child that shall be.

GOBBO I cannot think you are my son.

LAUNCELOT I know not what I shall think of that; but I
am Launcelot, the Jew's man, and I am sure Margery
your wife is my mother.

GOBBO Her name is Margery indeed! I'll be sworn, if
thou be Launcelot thou art mine own flesh and blood.
Lord worshipped might he be, what a beard hast thou   86
got! Thou hast got more hair on thy chin than Dobbin
my fill-horse has on his tail.   88

LAUNCELOT [rises] It should seem then that Dobbin's
tail grows backward. I am sure he had more hair of his
tail than I have of my face when I last saw him.

GOBBO Lord, how art thou changed! How dost thou and
thy master agree? I have brought him a present. How
'gree you now?

LAUNCELOT Well, well; but for mine own part, as I have
set up my rest to run away, so I will not rest till I have   96

86 *beard* (perhaps the old man's hand is on the back of Launcelot's head)
88 *fill-horse* cart horse   96 *set ... rest* i.e. determined

run some ground. My master 's a very Jew. Give him a
98 present? Give him a halter! I am famished in his ser-
99 vice; you may tell every finger I have with my ribs.
Father, I am glad you are come. Give me your present to
101 one Master Bassanio, who indeed gives rare new liveries.
If I serve not him, I will run as far as God has any
ground. O rare fortune, here comes the man! To him,
father, for I am a Jew if I serve the Jew any longer.

    Enter Bassanio, with [Leonardo and] a Follower or
    two.

BASSANIO You may do so, but let it be so hasted that
supper be ready at the farthest by five of the clock. See
these letters delivered, put the liveries to making, and
108 desire Gratiano to come anon to my lodging.

                 [Exit one of his men.]

LAUNCELOT To him, father!

GOBBO God bless your worship!

111 BASSANIO Gramercy. Wouldst thou aught with me?

GOBBO Here's my son, sir, a poor boy –

LAUNCELOT Not a poor boy, sir, but the rich Jew's man
that would, sir, as my father shall specify –

115 GOBBO He hath a great infection, sir, as one would say,
to serve –

LAUNCELOT Indeed, the short and the long is, I serve
the Jew, and have a desire, as my father shall specify –

GOBBO His master and he, saving your worship's rever-
120 ence, are scarce cater-cousins.

LAUNCELOT To be brief, the very truth is that the Jew
having done me wrong doth cause me, as my father,
123 being I hope an old man, shall frutify unto you –

GOBBO I have here a dish of doves that I would bestow
upon your worship, and my suit is –

---

98 *halter* hangman's noose 99 *tell* count 101 *liveries* costumes for
servants 108 *anon* presently, at once 111 *Gramercy* many thanks 115
infection (blunder for 'affection') 120 *cater-cousins* close friends 123
frutify (blunder for some word such as 'certify')

LAUNCELOT In very brief, the suit is impertinent to my- 126
self, as your worship shall know by this honest old man,
and though I say it, though old man, yet poor man, my
father.

BASSANIO One speak for both. What would you?

LAUNCELOT Serve you, sir.

GOBBO That is the very defect of the matter, sir. 131

BASSANIO
I know thee well; thou hast obtained thy suit.
Shylock thy master spoke with me this day,
And hath preferred thee, if it be preferment 134
To leave a rich Jew's service to become
The follower of so poor a gentleman.

LAUNCELOT The old proverb is very well parted be- 137
tween my master Shylock and you, sir. You have the
grace of God, sir, and he hath enough.

BASSANIO
Thou speak'st it well. Go, father, with thy son;
Take leave of thy old master and inquire
My lodging out. *[to a Servant]* Give him a livery
More guarded than his fellows'. See it done. 143

LAUNCELOT Father, in. I cannot get a service; no! I have
ne'er a tongue in my head; well! *[Looks at his palm.]* If
any man in Italy have a fairer table which doth offer to 146
swear upon a book – I shall have good fortune! Go to,
here's a simple line of life. Here's a small trifle of wives!
Alas, fifteen wives is nothing; eleven widows and nine
maids is a simple coming-in for one man. And then to
scape drowning thrice, and to be in peril of my life with
the edge of a feather-bed! Here are simple scapes. Well, 152
if Fortune be a woman, she's a good wench for this gear. 153

---

126 *impertinent* (blunder for 'pertinent')   131 *defect* (blunder for 'effect')
134 *preferred* recommended for advancement   137–39 *proverb . . . enough*
(play on the proverb 'He who has the grace of God has enough')   143
guarded decorated with braid   146 *table* palm of hand (Launcelot now
'reads' the lines of his palm)   152 *feather-bed* marriage bed (?); *scapes*
escapes   153 *this gear* these matters

Father, come. I'll take my leave of the Jew in the
twinkling.   *Exit Clown [Launcelot, with Old Gobbo].*

BASSANIO
I pray thee, good Leonardo, think on this:
These things being bought and orderly bestowed,
Return in haste, for I do feast to-night
My best-esteemed acquaintance. Hie thee, go.

LEONARDO
My best endeavors shall be done herein.
        Enter Gratiano.

GRATIANO
Where's your master?

LEONARDO   Yonder, sir, he walks.   *[Exit.]*

GRATIANO
Signior Bassanio!

BASSANIO   Gratiano!

GRATIANO
I have suit to you.

BASSANIO   You have obtained it.

GRATIANO You must not deny me. I must go with you
to Belmont.

BASSANIO
Why then you must. But hear thee, Gratiano:
Thou art too wild, too rude, and bold of voice –
168   Parts that become thee happily enough
And in such eyes as ours appear not faults;
But where thou art not known, why there they show
171   Something too liberal. Pray thee take pain
To allay with some cold drops of modesty
Thy skipping spirit, lest through thy wild behavior
174   I be misconst'red in the place I go to,
And lose my hopes.

GRATIANO   Signior Bassanio, hear me:
If I do not put on a sober habit,
Talk with respect, and swear but now and then,

168 *Parts* qualities   171 *liberal* free   174 *misconst'red* misunderstood

Wear prayer books in my pocket, look demurely –
Nay more, while grace is saying hood mine eyes   179
Thus with my hat, and sigh and say amen,
Use all the observance of civility   181
Like one well studied in a sad ostent   182
To please his grandam – never trust me more.

BASSANIO
Well, we shall see your bearing.

GRATIANO
Nay, but I bar to-night. You shall not gauge me   185
By what we do to-night.

BASSANIO   No, that were pity.
I would entreat you rather to put on
Your boldest suit of mirth, for we have friends
That purpose merriment. But fare you well ;
I have some business.

GRATIANO
And I must to Lorenzo and the rest,
But we will visit you at supper time.   *Exeunt*.

                        *

        Enter Jessica and [Launcelot] the Clown.   II, iii
JESSICA
I am sorry thou wilt leave my father so ;
Our house is hell, and thou a merry devil
Didst rob it of some taste of tediousness.
But fare thee well ; there is a ducat for thee.
And, Launcelot, soon at supper shalt thou see
Lorenzo, who is thy new master's guest.
Give him this letter ; do it secretly.
And so farewell ; I would not have my father
See me in talk with thee.

LAUNCELOT Adieu! Tears exhibit my tongue. Most 10

179 *hood* cover   181 *civility* polite behavior   182 *sad ostent* solemn appearance   185 *gauge* measure, judge
II, iii Within Shylock's house   10 *exhibit* (blunder for 'inhibit')

beautiful pagan, most sweet Jew! if a Christian did not
12 play the knave and get thee, I am much deceived. But
adieu! These foolish drops do something drown my
manly spirit. Adieu!

JESSICA
Farewell, good Launcelot.   *[Exit Launcelot.]*
Alack, what heinous sin is it in me
To be ashamed to be my father's child.
But though I am a daughter to his blood,
I am not to his manners. O Lorenzo,
If thou keep promise, I shall end this strife,
Become a Christian and thy loving wife!   *Exit.*

*

II, iv   *Enter Gratiano, Lorenzo, Salerio, and Solanio.*

LORENZO
Nay, we will slink away in supper time,
Disguise us at my lodging, and return
All in an hour.

GRATIANO
We have not made good preparation.

SALERIO
5   We have not spoke us yet of torchbearers.

SOLANIO
6   'Tis vile, unless it may be quaintly ordered,
And better in my mind not undertook.

LORENZO
'Tis now but four of clock. We have two hours
To furnish us.
          Enter Launcelot [with a letter].
                    Friend Launcelot, what's the news?

10 LAUNCELOT An it shall please you to break up this, it
shall seem to signify.

12 *get* beget
II, iv A public place   5 *spoke . . . torchbearers* ordered torchbearers   6
quaintly ordered nicely, or elaborately, arranged   10 *break up* break open

LORENZO

  I know the hand. In faith, 'tis a fair hand,
  And whiter than the paper it writ on
  Is the fair hand that writ.

GRATIANO   Love-news, in faith !

LAUNCELOT By your leave, sir.

LORENZO Whither goest thou ?

LAUNCELOT Marry, sir, to bid my old master the Jew to
  sup to-night with my new master the Christian.

LORENZO

  Hold here, take this. *[Gives money.]* Tell gentle Jessica
  I will not fail her. Speak it privately.   20
                          Exit Clown [Launcelot].
  Go, gentlemen ;
  Will you prepare you for this masque to-night ?
  I am provided of a torchbearer.

SALERIO

  Ay marry, I'll be gone about it straight.

SOLANIO

  And so will I.

LORENZO   Meet me and Gratiano

  At Gratiano's lodging some hour hence.

SALERIO

  'Tis good we do so.   *Exit [with Solanio].*

GRATIANO

  Was not that letter from fair Jessica ?

LORENZO

  I must needs tell thee all. She hath directed
  How I shall take her from her father's house,
  What gold and jewels she is furnished with,
  What page's suit she hath in readiness.
  If e'er the Jew her father come to heaven,
  It will be for his gentle daughter's sake ;   34
  And never dare misfortune cross her foot,   35
  Unless she do it under this excuse,   36

---

34 *gentle* (with pun on 'gentile'?)   **35** *never dare misfortune* may misfortune never dare   **36** *she* i.e. misfortune

37   That she is issue to a faithless Jew.
Come, go with me; peruse this as thou goest.
Fair Jessica shall be my torchbearer.

                           Exit [with Gratiano].

*

II, v   *Enter [Shylock the] Jew and [Launcelot,] his man*
              that was the Clown.

SHYLOCK
Well, thou shalt see, thy eyes shall be thy judge,
2   The difference of old Shylock and Bassanio –
What, Jessica! – Thou shalt not gormandize
As thou hast done with me – What, Jessica! –
And sleep, and snore, and rend apparel out –
Why, Jessica, I say!

LAUNCELOT   Why, Jessica!

SHYLOCK
Who bids thee call? I do not bid thee call.

LAUNCELOT Your worship was wont to tell me I could
do nothing without bidding.

       Enter Jessica.

JESSICA Call you? What is your will?

SHYLOCK
I am bid forth to supper, Jessica.
12   There are my keys. But wherefore should I go?
I am not bid for love – they flatter me –
But yet I'll go in hate to feed upon
The prodigal Christian. Jessica my girl,
Look to my house. I am right loath to go.
There is some ill a-brewing towards my rest,
18   For I did dream of money bags to-night.

   LAUNCELOT I beseech you, sir, go. My young master
20   doth expect your reproach.

---

37 *she* i.e. Jessica; *issue* offspring
II, v Before Shylock's house   **s.d.** *his . . . Clown* (perhaps originally
simply 'his man that was')   2 *of* between   12 *wherefore* why   18 *to-night*
last night   20 *reproach* (blunder for 'approach')

SHYLOCK So do I his.

LAUNCELOT And they have conspired together. I will not
   say you shall see a masque, but if you do, then it was not
   for nothing that my nose fell a-bleeding on Black Mon- 24
   day last at six o' clock i' th' morning, falling out that year 25
   on Ash Wednesday was four year in th' afternoon.

SHYLOCK
   What, are there masques? Hear you me, Jessica:
   Lock up my doors; and when you hear the drum
   And the vile squealing of the wry-necked fife, 29
   Clamber not you up to the casements then,
   Nor thrust your head into the public street
   To gaze on Christian fools with varnished faces; 32
   But stop my house's ears – I mean my casements;
   Let not the sound of shallow fopp'ry enter 34
   My sober house. By Jacob's staff I swear
   I have no mind of feasting forth to-night;
   But I will go. Go you before me, sirrah.
   Say I will come.

LAUNCELOT   I will go before, sir.
   Mistress, look out at window for all this:
        There will come a Christian by
        Will be worth a Jewess' eye.   *[Exit.]*

SHYLOCK
   What says that fool of Hagar's offspring? ha? 42

JESSICA
   His words were 'Farewell, mistress' – nothing else.

SHYLOCK
   The patch is kind enough, but a huge feeder, 44
   Snail-slow in profit, and he sleeps by day 45
   More than the wildcat. Drones hive not with me;
   Therefore I part with him, and part with him

---

24 *Black Monday* Easter Monday 25–26 *falling . . . afternoon* (Launcelot
departs into a gibberish of omens and fortunetelling) 29 *wry-necked fife*
i.e. played with the musician's head awry (?) 32 *varnished faces* painted
masks 34 *fopp'ry* frivolity 42 *Hagar's offspring* i.e. a gentile and an
outcast 44 *patch* fool 45 *profit* productive work

To one that I would have him help to waste
His borrowed purse. Well, Jessica, go in.
Perhaps I will return immediately.
Do as I bid you ; shut doors after you.
52 Fast bind, fast find –
A proverb never stale in thrifty mind.   *Exit.*

JESSICA
Farewell ; and if my fortune be not crost,
I have a father, you a daughter, lost.   *Exit.*

II, vi   *Enter the Masquers, Gratiano and Salerio.*

GRATIANO
1 This is the penthouse under which Lorenzo
Desired us to make stand.

SALERIO   His hour is almost past.

GRATIANO
And it is marvel he outdwells his hour,
For lovers ever run before the clock.

SALERIO
5 O ten times faster Venus' pigeons fly
To seal love's bonds new-made than they are wont
7 To keep obligèd faith unforfeited !

GRATIANO
That ever holds. Who riseth from a feast
With that keen appetite that he sits down ?
Where is the horse that doth untread again
His tedious measures with the unbated fire
That he did pace them first ? All things that are
Are with more spirit chasèd than enjoyed.
14 How like a younker or a prodigal
15 The scarfèd bark puts from her native bay,
Hugged and embracèd by the strumpet wind !
How like the prodigal doth she return,

52 *Fast* secure
II, vi 1 *penthouse* slanting eaves or shelter 5 *Venus' pigeons* doves
which draw Venus' chariot 7 *obligèd* bound by marriage or marriage
contract; *unforfeited* unbroken 14 *younker* youngster 15 *scarfèd* decked
with flags or streamers

With over-weathered ribs and ragged sails,
Lean, rent, and beggared by the strumpet wind !
   Enter Lorenzo.

SALERIO
Here comes Lorenzo ; more of this hereafter.

LORENZO
Sweet friends, your patience for my long abode.   21
Not I but my affairs have made you wait.
When you shall please to play the thieves for wives,   23
I'll watch as long for you then. Approach ;   24
Here dwells my father Jew. Ho ! who's within ?
   [Enter] Jessica above [in boy's clothes].

JESSICA
Who are you ? Tell me for more certainty,
Albeit I'll swear that I do know your tongue.

LORENZO
Lorenzo, and thy love.

JESSICA
Lorenzo certain, and my love indeed,
For who love I so much ? And now who knows
But you, Lorenzo, whether I am yours ?

LORENZO
Heaven and thy thoughts are witness that thou art.

JESSICA
Here, catch this casket ; it is worth the pains.
I am glad 'tis night – you do not look on me –
For I am much ashamed of my exchange.   35
But love is blind, and lovers cannot see
The pretty follies that themselves commit ;
For if they could, Cupid himself would blush
To see me thus transformèd to a boy.

LORENZO
Descend, for you must be my torchbearer.

JESSICA
What, must I hold a candle to my shames ?

21 *abode* delay   23 *play the thieves for* steal   24 *watch* wait   35 *exchange*
change of clothes

42   They in themselves, good sooth, are too too light.

43   Why, 'tis an office of discovery, love –
        And I should be obscured.

LORENZO   So are you, sweet,

45   Even in the lovely garnish of a boy.
        But come at once,

47   For the close night doth play the runaway,

48   And we are stayed for at Bassanio's feast.

JESSICA

        I will make fast the doors, and gild myself
        With some moe ducats, and be with you straight.

                                        [Exit above.]

GRATIANO

51   Now by my hood, a gentle and no Jew!

LORENZO

52   Beshrow me but I love her heartily!
        For she is wise, if I can judge of her,
        And fair she is, if that mine eyes be true,
        And true she is, as she hath proved herself;
        And therefore, like herself, wise, fair, and true,
        Shall she be placèd in my constant soul.

                Enter Jessica [below].

        What, art thou come? On, gentlemen, away!
        Our masquing mates by this time for us stay.

                        Exit [with Jessica and Salerio].

                Enter Antonio.

ANTONIO Who's there?

GRATIANO Signior Antonio?

ANTONIO

        Fie, fie, Gratiano! where are all the rest?
        'Tis nine o'clock; our friends all stay for you.

---

42 *light* frivolous, immodest (with pun) **43** *'tis ... discovery* i.e. torch-bearing is an act which reveals, sheds light upon **45** *garnish* dress, trimmings **47** *close* secret; *doth ... runaway* i.e. is passing rapidly **48** *stayed for* awaited **51** *gentle* gentile (with pun on 'gentle'?) **52** *Beshrow me* evil come to me (used lightly)

No masque to-night. The wind is come about;
Bassanio presently will go aboard.   65
I have sent twenty out to seek for you.

GRATIANO

I am glad on't. I desire no more delight
Than to be under sail and gone to-night.   *Exeunt.*

*

[*Flourish of cornets.*] *Enter Portia with Morocco and* II, vii
both their Trains.

PORTIA

Go, draw aside the curtains and discover   1
The several caskets to this noble Prince.
Now make your choice.

MOROCCO

This first, of gold, who this inscription bears,
'Who chooseth me shall gain what many men desire';
The second, silver, which this promise carries,
'Who chooseth me shall get as much as he deserves';
This third, dull lead, with warning all as blunt,
'Who chooseth me must give and hazard all he hath.' 9
How shall I know if I do choose the right?

PORTIA

The one of them contains my picture, Prince.
If you choose that, then I am yours withal.

MOROCCO

Some god direct my judgment! Let me see –
I will survey th' inscriptions back again.
What says this leaden casket?
'Who chooseth me must give and hazard all he hath.'
Must give – for what? for lead! hazard for lead?
This casket threatens; men that hazard all

65 *presently* immediately
II, vii Within Portia's house in Belmont   1 *discover* reveal   9 *hazard* risk,
gamble

Do it in hope of fair advantages.
A golden mind stoops not to shows of dross;
21   I'll then nor give nor hazard aught for lead.
What says the silver with her virgin hue?
'Who chooseth me shall get as much as he deserves.'
As much as he deserves? Pause there, Morocco,
And weigh thy value with an even hand:
26   If thou be'st rated by thy estimation,
Thou dost deserve enough; and yet enough
May not extend so far as to the lady;
And yet to be afeard of my deserving
30   Were but a weak disabling of myself.
As much as I deserve? Why that's the lady!
I do in birth deserve her, and in fortunes,
In graces, and in qualities of breeding;
But more than these, in love I do deserve.
What if I strayed no farther, but chose here?
Let's see once more this saying graved in gold:
'Who chooseth me shall gain what many men desire.'
Why that's the lady! All the world desires her;
From the four corners of the earth they come
40   To kiss this shrine, this mortal breathing saint.
The Hyrcanian deserts and the vasty wilds
Of wide Arabia are as throughfares now
For princes to come view fair Portia.
The watery kingdom, whose ambitious head
Spits in the face of heaven, is no bar
To stop the foreign spirits, but they come
As o'er a brook to see fair Portia.
One of these three contains her heavenly picture.
Is't like that lead contains her? 'Twere damnation
50   To think so base a thought; it were too gross
51   To rib her cerecloth in the obscure grave.
Or shall I think in silver she's immured,

21 *nor give* neither give   26 *estimation* reputation (?), worth (?)   30 *disabling* underrating   50 *it* i.e. lead   51 *rib* cover, enclose; *cerecloth* waxed cloth used in wrapping for burial

Being ten times undervalued to tried gold?
O sinful thought! Never so rich a gem
Was set in worse than gold. They have in England
A coin that bears the figure of an angel
Stamped in gold – but that's insculped upon;   57
But here an angel in a golden bed
Lies all within. Deliver me the key.
Here do I choose, and thrive I as I may!

PORTIA
There, take it, Prince; and if my form lie there,
Then I am yours.
    [He opens the golden casket.]

MOROCCO   O hell! what have we here?
A carrion Death, within whose empty eye   63
There is a written scroll! I'll read the writing.
    'All that glisters is not gold;   65
    Often have you heard that told.
    Many a man his life hath sold
    But my outside to behold.   68
    Gilded tombs do worms infold.
    Had you been as wise as bold,
    Young in limbs, in judgment old,
    Your answer had not been inscrolled.   72
    Fare you well, your suit is cold.'
Cold indeed, and labor lost.
Then farewell heat, and welcome frost!
Portia, adieu. I have too grieved a heart
To take a tedious leave. Thus losers part.
      Exit [with his Train. Flourish of cornets].

PORTIA
A gentle riddance. Draw the curtains, go.
Let all of his complexion choose me so.   *Exeunt.*

*

57 *insculped upon* engraved on the surface   63 *Death* death's-head, skull
65 *glisters* glitters   68 *my outside* i.e. my shining surface   72 *inscrolled* thus
inscribed

II, viii   *Enter Salerio and Solanio.*

SALERIO

Why, man, I saw Bassanio under sail;
With him is Gratiano gone along,
And in their ship I am sure Lorenzo is not.

SOLANIO

The villain Jew with outcries raised the Duke,
Who went with him to search Bassanio's ship.

SALERIO

He came too late – the ship was under sail,
But there the Duke was given to understand
That in a gondola were seen together
Lorenzo and his amorous Jessica.

10   Besides, Antonio certified the Duke
They were not with Bassanio in his ship.

SOLANIO

I never heard a passion so confused,
So strange, outrageous, and so variable
As the dog Jew did utter in the streets:
'My daughter! O my ducats! O my daughter!
Fled with a Christian! O my Christian ducats!
Justice! the law! my ducats and my daughter!
A sealèd bag, two sealèd bags of ducats,
Of double ducats, stol'n from me by my daughter!
And jewels – two stones, two rich and precious stones,
Stol'n by my daughter! Justice! Find the girl!
She hath the stones upon her, and the ducats!'

SALERIO

Why, all the boys in Venice follow him,
Crying his stones, his daughter, and his ducats.

SOLANIO

25   Let good Antonio look he keep his day,
Or he shall pay for this.

SALERIO   Marry, well rememb'red.

27   I reasoned with a Frenchman yesterday,

II, viii A street in Venice   25 *keep his day* repay his debt on the day agreed
27 *reasoned* talked

Who told me, in the narrow seas that part
The French and English there miscarrièd
A vessel of our country richly fraught.   30
I thought upon Antonio when he told me,
And wished in silence that it were not his.

SOLANIO
You were best to tell Antonio what you hear.
Yet do not suddenly, for it may grieve him.

SALERIO
A kinder gentleman treads not the earth.
I saw Bassanio and Antonio part :
Bassanio told him he would make some speed
Of his return ; he answered, 'Do not so.
Slubber not business for my sake, Bassanio,   39
But stay the very riping of the time ;
And for the Jew's bond which he hath of me,
Let it not enter in your mind of love.   42
Be merry, and employ your chiefest thoughts
To courtship and such fair ostents of love   44
As shall conveniently become you there.'
And even there, his eye being big with tears,
Turning his face, he put his hand behind him,
And with affection wondrous sensible   48
He wrung Bassanio's hand ; and so they parted.

SOLANIO
I think he only loves the world for him.
I pray thee let us go and find him out,
And quicken his embracèd heaviness   52
With some delight or other.
SALERIO   Do we so.   *Exeunt.*

*

30 *fraught* laden   39 *Slubber* perform hastily, botch   42 *mind of love*
thoughts of wooing   44 *ostents* shows   48 *wondrous sensible* wonderfully
strong in feeling   52 *quicken . . . heaviness* enliven the sadness he has em-
braced

II, ix   *Enter Nerissa and a Servitor.*

NERISSA

1   Quick, quick I pray thee ! draw the curtain straight.
     The Prince of Arragon hath ta'en his oath,
3   And comes to his election presently.
          [Flourish of cornets.] Enter Arragon, his Train, and
          Portia.

PORTIA

     Behold, there stand the caskets, noble Prince.
     If you choose that wherein I am contained,
     Straight shall our nuptial rites be solemnized ;
     But if you fail, without more speech, my lord,
     You must be gone from hence immediately.

ARRAGON

     I am enjoined by oath to observe three things :
     First, never to unfold to any one
     Which casket 'twas I chose ; next, if I fail
     Of the right casket, never in my life
     To woo a maid in way of marriage ;
     Lastly, if I do fail in fortune of my choice,
     Immediately to leave you and be gone.

PORTIA

     To these injunctions every one doth swear
     That comes to hazard for my worthless self.

ARRAGON

18   And so have I addressed me. Fortune now
     To my heart's hope ! Gold, silver, and base lead.
     'Who chooseth me must give and hazard all he hath.'
21   You shall look fairer ere I give or hazard.
     What says the golden chest ? Ha, let me see !
     'Who chooseth me shall gain what many men desire.'
24   What many men desire – that 'many' may be meant
     By the fool multitude that choose by show,

II, ix Within Portia's house in Belmont   1 *straight* at once   3 *election*
choice; *presently* immediately   18 *addressed me* prepared myself, i.e. by
thus swearing   21 *You . . . hazard* (addressed to the leaden casket)   24–25
meant By intended to mean, to suggest

Not learning more than the fond eye doth teach, 26
Which pries not to th' interior, but like the martlet 27
Builds in the weather on the outward wall, 28
Even in the force and road of casualty. 29
I will not choose what many men desire,
Because I will not jump with common spirits
And rank me with the barbarous multitudes.
Why then, to thee, thou silver treasure house!
Tell me once more what title thou dost bear.
'Who chooseth me shall get as much as he deserves.'
And well said too, for who shall go about
To cozen fortune, and be honorable 37
Without the stamp of merit? Let none presume
To wear an undeservèd dignity.
O that estates, degrees, and offices 40
Were not derived corruptly, and that clear honor
Were purchased by the merit of the wearer!
How many then should cover that stand bare, 43
How many be commanded that command;
How much low peasantry would then be gleaned 45
From the true seed of honor, and how much honor 46
Picked from the chaff and ruin of the times
To be new varnished. Well, but to my choice. 48
'Who chooseth me shall get as much as he deserves.'
I will assume desert. Give me a key for this,
And instantly unlock my fortunes here.
        [He opens the silver casket.]

PORTIA
Too long a pause for that which you find there.

ARRAGON
What's here? The portrait of a blinking idiot
Presenting me a schedule! I will read it. 54

---

26 *fond* foolish   **27** *martlet* a bird   **28** *in* exposed to   **29** *force . . . casualty* power and path of mishap   **37** *cozen* cheat   **40** *estates, degrees* social ranks   **43** *cover . . . bare* wear hats who now stand bareheaded   **45** *gleaned* culled   **46** *honor* noble rank   **48** *new varnished* refurbished   **54** *schedule* scroll

How much unlike art thou to Portia !
How much unlike my hopes and my deservings !
'Who chooseth me shall have as much as he deserves.'
Did I deserve no more than a fool's head ?
Is that my prize ? Are my deserts no better ?

PORTIA

60   To offend and judge are distinct offices,
     And of opposèd natures.

ARRAGON   What is here ?

62   'The fire seven times tried this ;
            Seven times tried that judgment is
            That did never choose amiss.
            Some there be that shadows kiss ;
            Such have but a shadow's bliss.
67   There be fools alive iwis,
            Silvered o'er, and so was this.
            Take what wife you will to bed,
            I will ever be your head.
71   So be gone ; you are sped.'
     Still more fool I shall appear
     By the time I linger here.
     With one fool's head I came to woo,
     But I go away with two.
     Sweet, adieu. I'll keep my oath,
77   Patiently to bear my wroath.   *[Exit with his Train.]*

PORTIA

     Thus hath the candle singed the moth.
     O these deliberate fools ! When they do choose,
     They have the wisdom by their wit to lose.

NERISSA

     The ancient saying is no heresy :
     Hanging and wiving goes by destiny.

PORTIA

     Come draw the curtain, Nerissa.

60–61 *To offend . . . natures* i.e. those who are subject to judgment may not
be their own judges   62 *tried* tested (?), purified (?)   67 *iwis* certainly
71 *sped* done for   77 *wroath* disappointment (?), resentment (?)

Enter Messenger.

MESSENGER
  Where is my lady?
PORTIA   Here. What would my lord?
MESSENGER
  Madam, there is alighted at your gate
  A young Venetian, one that comes before
  To signify th' approaching of his lord,
  From whom he bringeth sensible regreets,   88
  To wit, besides commends and courteous breath,
  Gifts of rich value. Yet I have not seen
  So likely an ambassador of love.
  A day in April never came so sweet
  To show how costly summer was at hand,   93
  As this fore-spurrer comes before his lord.   94
PORTIA
  No more, I pray thee. I am half afeard
  Thou wilt say anon he is some kin to thee,
  Thou spend'st such high-day wit in praising him.   97
  Come, come, Nerissa, for I long to see
  Quick Cupid's post that comes so mannerly.   99
NERISSA
  Bassanio, Lord Love, if thy will it be!   *Exeunt.* 100

*

[Enter] Solanio and Salerio.   III, i
SOLANIO Now what news on the Rialto?
SALERIO Why, yet it lives there unchecked that Antonio 2
  hath a ship of rich lading wracked on the narrow seas –
  the Goodwins I think they call the place, a very danger- 4
  ous flat, and fatal, where the carcasses of many a tall ship

88 *sensible regreets* tangible greetings, i.e. more than words 93 *costly* rich,
bountiful 94 *fore-spurrer* forerunner 97 *high-day* holiday, i.e. suitable
for a special occasion 99 *post* messenger 100 *Lord Love* god of love, i.e.
Cupid
III, i A street in Venice 2 *lives* i.e. circulates; *unchecked* without denial
(?), extensively (?) 4 *Goodwins* Goodwin Sands (off the English coast)

6 lie buried as they say, if my gossip Report be an honest
woman of her word.

SOLANIO I would she were as lying a gossip in that as ever
9 knapped ginger or made her neighbors believe she wept
for the death of a third husband. But it is true, without
11 any slips of prolixity or crossing the plain highway of talk,
that the good Antonio, the honest Antonio – O that I
had a title good enough to keep his name company! –

14 SALERIO Come, the full stop!

SOLANIO Ha, what sayest thou? Why the end is, he hath
lost a ship.

SALERIO I would it might prove the end of his losses.

18 SOLANIO Let me say amen betimes lest the devil cross
my prayer, for here he comes in the likeness of a Jew.
        Enter Shylock.
How now, Shylock? What news among the merchants?

SHYLOCK You knew, none so well, none so well as you, of
my daughter's flight.

SALERIO That's certain. I for my part knew the tailor
24 that made the wings she flew withal.

SOLANIO And Shylock for his own part knew the bird
26 was fledge, and then it is the complexion of them all to
27 leave the dam.

SHYLOCK She is damned for it.

SALERIO That's certain, if the devil may be her judge.

SHYLOCK My own flesh and blood to rebel!

31 SOLANIO Out upon it, old carrion! Rebels it at these
years?

SHYLOCK I say my daughter is my flesh and my blood.

SALERIO There is more difference between thy flesh and
hers than between jet and ivory, more between your
bloods than there is between red wine and Rhenish. But

---

6 *gossip Report* i.e. Dame Rumor   9 *knapped* nibbled   11 *slips of prolixity* lapses into wordiness; *crossing . . . talk* i.e. deviation from plain
speech   14 *full step* period, end of statement   18 *cross* thwart   24 *wings*
i.e. the boy's suit (with pun on *flight*)   26 *fledge* ready to fly; *complexion*
disposition   27 *dam* mother, i.e. parent   31 *carrion* dead, putrefied
flesh   31–32 *Rebels . . . years* i.e. do you have fleshly desires at your age

tell us, do you hear whether Antonio have had any loss at sea or no?

SHYLOCK There I have another bad match! A bankrout, 38 a prodigal, who dare scarce show his head on the Rialto, a beggar that was used to come so smug upon the mart! 40 Let him look to his bond. He was wont to call me usurer. Let him look to his bond. He was wont to lend money for a Christian cursy. Let him look to his bond. 43

SALERIO Why, I am sure if he forfeit thou wilt not take his flesh. What's that good for?

SHYLOCK To bait fish withal. If it will feed nothing else, it will feed my revenge. He hath disgraced me and hind'red me half a million, laughed at my losses, mocked at my gains, scorned my nation, thwarted my bargains, cooled my friends, heated mine enemies—and what's his reason? I am a Jew. Hath not a Jew eyes? Hath not a Jew hands, organs, dimensions, senses, affections, passions? – fed 52 with the same food, hurt with the same weapons, subject to the same diseases, healed by the same means, warmed and cooled by the same winter and summer as a Christian is? If you prick us, do we not bleed? If you tickle us, do we not laugh? If you poison us, do we not die? And if you wrong us, shall we not revenge? If we are like you in the rest, we will resemble you in that. If a Jew wrong a Christian, what is his humility? Revenge. If a Christian 60 wrong a Jew, what should his sufferance be by Christian 61 example? Why revenge! The villainy you teach me I will execute, and it shall go hard but I will better the instruction.

Enter a Man from Antonio.

MAN Gentlemen, my master Antonio is at his house and desires to speak with you both.

SALERIO We have been up and down to seek him.

Enter Tubal.

---

38 *match* bargain; *bankrout* bankrupt   40 *mart* market place, exchange   43 *for . . . cursy* as a Christian courtesy   52 *dimensions* bodily members, form   60 *his* i.e. the Christian's   61 *his* i.e. the Jew's

68 SOLANIO Here comes another of the tribe. A third cannot
be matched, unless the devil himself turn Jew.

> *Exeunt [Solanio, Salerio, and Man].*

SHYLOCK How now, Tubal! What news from Genoa?
Hast thou found my daughter?

TUBAL I often came where I did hear of her, but cannot
find her.

SHYLOCK Why there, there, there, there! A diamond gone
75 cost me two thousand ducats in Frankford! The curse
never fell upon our nation till now; I never felt it till
now. Two thousand ducats in that, and other precious,
precious jewels. I would my daughter were dead at my
foot, and the jewels in her ear! Would she were hearsed
at my foot, and the ducats in her coffin! No news of
them, why so? – and I know not what's spent in the
search. Why thou loss upon loss! the thief gone with so
much, and so much to find the thief! – and no satisfac-
tion, no revenge! nor no ill luck stirring but what lights
o' my shoulders, no sighs but o' my breathing, no tears
but o' my shedding.

TUBAL Yes, other men have ill luck too. Antonio, as I
heard in Genoa –

SHYLOCK What, what, what? Ill luck, ill luck?

90 TUBAL Hath an argosy cast away coming from Tripolis.

SHYLOCK I thank God, I thank God! Is it true? is it true?

TUBAL I spoke with some of the sailors that escaped the
wrack.

SHYLOCK I thank thee, good Tubal. Good news, good
news! Ha, ha! Heard in Genoa?

TUBAL Your daughter spent in Genoa, as I heard, one
night fourscore ducats.

SHYLOCK Thou stick'st a dagger in me. I shall never see
my gold again. Fourscore ducats at a sitting, fourscore
ducats!

68–69 *cannot be matched* cannot be found to match them   75 *Frankford*
Frankfort

TUBAL There came divers of Antonio's creditors in my   100
  company to Venice that swear he cannot choose but
  break.   102

SHYLOCK I am very glad of it. I'll plague him; I'll torture
  him. I am glad of it.

TUBAL One of them showed me a ring that he had of your
  daughter for a monkey.

SHYLOCK Out upon her! Thou torturest me, Tubal. It
  was my turquoise; I had it of Leah when I was a   107
  bachelor. I would not have given it for a wilderness
  of monkeys.

TUBAL But Antonio is certainly undone.

SHYLOCK Nay, that's true, that's very true. Go, Tubal, fee   110
  me an officer; bespeak him a fortnight before. I will   111
  have the heart of him if he forfeit, for were he out of
  Venice I can make what merchandise I will. Go, Tubal,   113
  and meet me at our synagogue; go, good Tubal; at our
  synagogue, Tubal.   *Exeunt.*

*

Enter Bassanio, Portia, Gratiano, [Nerissa,] and all III, ii
  their Trains.

PORTIA

I pray you tarry; pause a day or two
Before you hazard, for in choosing wrong
I lose your company. Therefore forbear awhile.
There's something tells me, but it is not love,
I would not lose you; and you know yourself
Hate counsels not in such a quality.   6
But lest you should not understand me well –
And yet a maiden hath no tongue but thought –

---

100 *divers* various, several 102 *break* go bankrupt 107 *Leah* Shylock's
wife 110 *fee* hire 111 *officer* arresting officer; *bespeak* engage 113 *make*
. . . *will* drive what bargains I wish
III, ii Within Portia's house in Belmont 6 *quality* way

I would detain you here some month or two
Before you venture for me. I could teach you
11 How to choose right, but then I am forsworn.
So will I never be. So may you miss me.
But if you do, you'll make me wish a sin –
That I had been forsworn. Beshrow your eyes!
15 They have o'erlooked me and divided me;
One half of me is yours, the other half yours –
Mine own I would say; but if mine then yours,
18 And so all yours! O these naughty times
Puts bars between the owners and their rights!
20 And so, though yours, not yours. Prove it so,
Let fortune go to hell for it, not I.
22 I speak too long, but 'tis to peize the time,
23 To eke it and to draw it out in length,
To stay you from election.

BASSANIO   Let me choose,
25 For as I am, I live upon the rack.

PORTIA
Upon the rack, Bassanio? Then confess
What treason there is mingled with your love.

BASSANIO
None but that ugly treason of mistrust
Which makes me fear th' enjoying of my love.
There may as well be amity and life
'Tween snow and fire, as treason and my love.

PORTIA
Ay, but I fear you speak upon the rack,
Where men enforcèd do speak anything.

BASSANIO
Promise me life and I'll confess the truth.

PORTIA
Well then, confess and live.

---

11 *forsworn* false to my oath   15 *o'erlooked* bewitched   18 *naughty* evil,
worthless   20 *Prove it so* if it prove so   22 *peize* retard (?), augment, fill in
(?)   23 *eke* increase   25–27 *upon the rack . . . treason* (refers to confessions
of treason obtained by torture on the rack)

BASSANIO   Confess and love   35
　　　Had been the very sum of my confession!
　　　O happy torment, when my torturer
　　　Doth teach me answers for deliverance.   38
　　　But let me to my fortune and the caskets.

PORTIA
　　　Away then! I am locked in one of them;
　　　If you do love me, you will find me out.
　　　Nerissa and the rest, stand all aloof.
　　　Let music sound while he doth make his choice;
　　　Then if he lose he makes a swanlike end,   44
　　　Fading in music. That the comparison   45
　　　May stand more proper, my eye shall be the stream
　　　And wat'ry deathbed for him. He may win;
　　　And what is music then? Then music is
　　　Even as the flourish when true subjects bow   49
　　　To a new-crownèd monarch. Such it is
　　　As are those dulcet sounds in break of day
　　　That creep into the dreaming bridegroom's ear
　　　And summon him to marriage. Now he goes,
　　　With no less presence but with much more love
　　　Than young Alcides when he did redeem   55
　　　The virgin tribute paid by howling Troy
　　　To the sea monster. I stand for sacrifice;   57
　　　The rest aloof are the Dardanian wives,   58
　　　With blearèd visages come forth to view   59
　　　The issue of th' exploit. Go, Hercules!   60
　　　Live thou, I live. With much, much more dismay   61
　　　I view the fight than thou that mak'st the fray.

35–36 *Confess . . . confession* i.e. why, as for my confession, love would have been the gist of it (Bassanio leaps to this with a play on the words 'live' and 'love')　38 *answers for deliverance* answers that will obtain release　44 *swanlike end* (the swan was thought to sing just before death)　45 *comparison* figure, metaphor　49 *flourish* sounding of trumpets　55–57 *Alcides . . . monster* (Alcides, or Hercules, rescued the daughter of the Trojan king from sacrifice to a sea monster)　57 *stand for sacrifice* represent the sacrificial victim　58 *Dardanian* Trojan　59 *blearèd* i.e. weeping　60 *issue* outcome　61 *Live thou* if you live

A song the whilst Bassanio comments on the caskets to himself.

63   Tell me where is fancy bred,
Or in the heart, or in the head?
How begot, how nourishèd?
    Reply, reply.
It is engend'red in the eyes,
With gazing fed, and fancy dies
In the cradle where it lies.
    Let us all ring fancy's knell.
    I'll begin it – Ding, dong, bell.

ALL   Ding, dong, bell.

BASSANIO

73   So may the outward shows be least themselves;
The world is still deceived with ornament.
In law, what plea so tainted and corrupt
76   But being seasoned with a gracious voice,
Obscures the show of evil? In religion,
What damnèd error but some sober brow
Will bless it and approve it with a text,
Hiding the grossness with fair ornament?
81   There is no vice so simple but assumes
Some mark of virtue on his outward parts.
How many cowards whose hearts are all as false
As stairs of sand, wear yet upon their chins
The beards of Hercules and frowning Mars,
86   Who inward searched, have livers white as milk!
87   And these assume but valor's excrement
88   To render them redoubted. Look on beauty,
And you shall see 'tis purchased by the weight,
Which therein works a miracle in nature,
91   Making them lightest that wear most of it:

63 *fancy* fond love, infatuation   73 *be least themselves* i.e. belie the inner quality   76 *seasoned* spiced   81 *simple* unadulterated   86 *livers . . . milk* (cowards were supposed to have white livers)   87 *excrement* outer growth (as hair)   88 *redoubted* feared   91 *lightest* (with pun on 'light' in the sense of 'light woman')

So are those crispèd snaky golden locks,   92
Which maketh such wanton gambols with the wind
Upon supposèd fairness, often known   94
To be the dowry of a second head,   95
The skull that bred them in the sepulchre.
Thus ornament is but the guilèd shore   97
To a most dangerous sea, the beauteous scarf
Veiling an Indian beauty; in a word,   99
The seeming truth which cunning times put on
To entrap the wisest. Therefore then, thou gaudy gold,
Hard food for Midas, I will none of thee;   102
Nor none of thee, thou pale and common drudge   103
'Tween man and man. But thou, thou meagre lead
Which rather threaten'st than dost promise aught,
Thy paleness moves me more than eloquence;
And here choose I. Joy be the consequence!

PORTIA *[aside]*
How all the other passions fleet to air:
As doubtful thoughts, and rash-embraced despair,   109
And shudd'ring fear, and green-eyed jealousy.
O love, be moderate, allay thy ecstasy,
In measure rain thy joy, scant this excess!   112
I feel too much thy blessing. Make it less
For fear I surfeit.

BASSANIO *[opening the leaden casket]*
                    What find I here?
Fair Portia's counterfeit! What demigod   115
Hath come so near creation? Move these eyes?
Or whether, riding on the balls of mine,   117
Seem they in motion? Here are severed lips
Parted with sugar breath; so sweet a bar

92 *crispèd* curled 94 *Upon supposèd fairness* on the head of a supposed
beauty 95–96 *dowry . . . sepulchre* i.e. hair taken from a person now dead
and buried 97 *guilèd* beguiling 99 *Indian* i.e. swarthy, not fair 102
Midas (all that Midas touched, including food, turned to gold) 103–04
pale . . . and man i.e. silver 109 *As* such as 112 *scant* lessen 115 *counterfeit* image, portrait 115–16 *What demigod . . . creation* i.e. only a demigod
could have painted such a lifelike picture 117 *Or whether* or

77

120 Should sunder such sweet friends. Here in her hairs
The painter plays the spider, and hath woven
A golden mesh t' entrap the hearts of men
123 Faster than gnats in cobwebs. But her eyes –
How could he see to do them? Having made one,
Methinks it should have power to steal both his
126 And leave itself unfurnished. Yet look, how far
127 The substance of my praise doth wrong this shadow
In underprizing it, so far this shadow
129 Doth limp behind the substance. Here's the scroll,
130 The continent and summary of my fortune.
        'You that choose not by the view
132   Chance as fair, and choose as true.
        Since this fortune falls to you,
        Be content and seek no new.
        If you be well pleased with this
        And hold your fortune for your bliss,
        Turn you where your lady is,
        And claim her with a loving kiss.'
A gentle scroll. Fair lady, by your leave.
    [Kisses her.]
140 I come by note, to give and to receive.
Like one of two contending in a prize,
That thinks he hath done well in people's eyes,
Hearing applause and universal shout,
Giddy in spirit, still gazing in a doubt
145 Whether those peals of praise be his or no –
So, thrice-fair lady, stand I even so,
As doubtful whether what I see be true,
Until confirmed, signed, ratified by you.

PORTIA
You see me, Lord Bassanio, where I stand,

---

120 *sweet friends* i.e. the two lips   **123** *Faster* more securely   **126** *unfurnished* i.e. without the other eye, since the painter could not see to paint it   **127** *shadow* picture   **129** *substance* i.e. the real Portia   **130** *continent* container   **132** *Chance as fair* hazard as fortunately   **140** *come by note* come according to directions of the scroll (?), present my bill for payment (?)   **145** *his* addressed to him

Such as I am. Though for myself alone
I would not be ambitious in my wish
To wish myself much better, yet for you
I would be trebled twenty times myself,
A thousand times more fair, ten thousand times more
    rich,
That only to stand high in your account,   155
I might in virtues, beauties, livings, friends,
Exceed account. But the full sum of me
Is sum of something – which, to term in gross,   158
Is an unlessoned girl, unschooled, unpractised;
Happy in this, she is not yet so old
But she may learn; happier than this,
She is not bred so dull but she can learn;
Happiest of all, is that her gentle spirit
Commits itself to yours to be directed,
As from her lord, her governor, her king.   165
Myself and what is mine to you and yours
Is now converted. But now I was the lord   167
Of this fair mansion, master of my servants,
Queen o'er myself; and even now, but now,
This house, these servants, and this same myself
Are yours, my lord's. I give them with this ring,
Which when you part from, lose, or give away,
Let it presage the ruin of your love
And be my vantage to exclaim on you.   174

BASSANIO
Madam, you have bereft me of all words.
Only my blood speaks to you in my veins,
And there is such confusion in my powers   177
As, after some oration fairly spoke
By a belovèd prince, there doth appear
Among the buzzing pleasèd multitude,

---

155 *That* so that; *account* estimation   158 *something* i.e. at least something;
term in gross state in full   165 *from* by   167 *converted* transferred; *But now*
a moment ago   174 *vantage . . . you* opportunity to reproach you   177
powers faculties

Where every something being blent together
Turns to a wild of nothing, save of joy
Expressed and not expressed. But when this ring
Parts from this finger, then parts life from hence;
O then be bold to say Bassanio's dead!

NERISSA

My lord and lady, it is now our time,
187 That have stood by and seen our wishes prosper,
To cry 'good joy.' Good joy, my lord and lady!

GRATIANO

My Lord Bassanio, and my gentle lady,
I wish you all the joy that you can wish –
For I am sure you can wish none from me;
And when your honors mean to solemnize
The bargain of your faith, I do beseech you
Even at that time I may be married too.

BASSANIO

195 With all my heart, so thou canst get a wife.

GRATIANO

I thank your lordship; you have got me one.
My eyes, my lord, can look as swift as yours:
You saw the mistress, I beheld the maid.
199 You loved, I loved; for intermission
No more pertains to me, my lord, than you.
Your fortune stood upon the caskets there,
And so did mine too, as the matter falls;
203 For wooing here until I sweat again,
204 And swearing till my very roof was dry
205 With oaths of love, at last – if promise last –
I got a promise of this fair one here
To have her love, provided that your fortune
Achieved her mistress.

PORTIA   Is this true, Nerissa?

187 *That* who 195 *so* if 199 *intermission* delay, inactivity 203 *again*
repeatedly 204 *roof* (of the mouth) 205 *if promise last* i.e. if Nerissa's
promise is still good

NERISSA
    Madam, it is, so you stand pleased withal. 209

BASSANIO
    And do you, Gratiano, mean good faith?

GRATIANO Yes, faith, my lord.

BASSANIO
    Our feast shall be much honored in your marriage.

GRATIANO We'll play with them the first boy for a thou- 213
sand ducats.

NERISSA What, and stake down? 215

GRATIANO No, we shall ne'er win at that sport, and stake 216
down.

    But who comes here? Lorenzo and his infidel! 218
    What, and my old Venetian friend Salerio!
        Enter Lorenzo, Jessica, and Salerio, a Messenger
        from Venice.

BASSANIO
    Lorenzo and Salerio, welcome hither,
    If that the youth of my new int'rest here 221
    Have power to bid you welcome. By your leave,
    I bid my very friends and countrymen,
    Sweet Portia, welcome.

PORTIA   So do I, my lord.
    They are entirely welcome.

LORENZO
    I thank your honor. For my part, my lord,
    My purpose was not to have seen you here,
    But meeting with Salerio by the way,
    He did entreat me past all saying nay
    To come with him along.

SALERIO   I did, my lord,
    And I have reason for it. Signior Antonio

---

209 *so . . . withal* if it pleases you   213–14 *play . . . ducats* wager a thousand
ducats, the couple having the first boy to be the winner   215 *stake down* bets
made with cash down   216–17 *stake down* (with ribald pun)   218 *infidel*
i.e. Jessica   221 *int'rest* position in the household

232   Commends him to you.
>   *[Gives Bassanio a letter.]*

BASSANIO   Ere I ope his letter,
I pray you tell me how my good friend doth.

SALERIO
Not sick, my lord, unless it be in mind,
Nor well unless in mind. His letters there
236   Will show you his estate.
>   *Open the letter.*

GRATIANO
Nerissa, cheer yond stranger; bid her welcome.
Your hand, Salerio. What's the news from Venice?
239   How doth that royal merchant, good Antonio?
I know he will be glad of our success;
241   We are the Jasons, we have won the Fleece.

SALERIO
I would you had won the fleece that he hath lost!

PORTIA
243   There are some shrowd contents in yond same paper
That steals the color from Bassanio's cheek:
Some dear friend dead, else nothing in the world
Could turn so much the constitution
Of any constant man. What, worse and worse?
With leave, Bassanio – I am half yourself,
And I must freely have the half of anything
That this same paper brings you.

BASSANIO   O sweet Portia,
Here are a few of the unpleasant'st words
That ever blotted paper! Gentle lady,
When I did first impart my love to you,
I freely told you all the wealth I had
Ran in my veins – I was a gentleman –

---

232 *Commends him* sends his greetings   236 *estate* condition, state of affairs
239 *royal merchant* merchant of great affluence ('merchant prince'); sometimes one engaged in royal employment   241 *Jasons . . . Fleece* (see I, i, 170–72)   243 *shrowd* cursed, bitter

And then I told you true; and yet, dear lady,
Rating myself at nothing, you shall see
How much I was a braggart. When I told you
My state was nothing, I should then have told you   259
That I was worse than nothing; for indeed
I have engaged myself to a dear friend,   261
Engaged my friend to his mere enemy   262
To feed my means. Here is a letter, lady,
The paper as the body of my friend,
And every word in it a gaping wound
Issuing lifeblood. But is it true, Salerio?
Hath all his ventures failed? What, not one hit?
From Tripolis, from Mexico and England,
From Lisbon, Barbary, and India,
And not one vessel scape the dreadful touch
Of merchant-marring rocks?   271

SALERIO   Not one, my lord.
Besides, it should appear that if he had
The present money to discharge the Jew,   273
He would not take it. Never did I know   274
A creature that did bear the shape of man
So keen and greedy to confound a man.   276
He plies the Duke at morning and at night,
And doth impeach the freedom of the state   278
If they deny him justice. Twenty merchants,
The Duke himself, and the magnificoes   280
Of greatest port have all persuaded with him,   281
But none can drive him from the envious plea   282
Of forfeiture, of justice, and his bond.

JESSICA
When I was with him, I have heard him swear

259 *state* estate, property   261 *engaged myself* become indebted   262 *mere*
unqualified, sheer   271 *merchant* merchant ship   273 *discharge* pay off
274 *He* i.e. the Jew   276 *confound* ruin   278 *freedom . . . state* freedom of
commerce, of contract, in Venice   280 *magnificoes* Venetian magnates
281 *port* dignity   282 *envious* malicious

To Tubal and to Chus, his countrymen,
That he would rather have Antonio's flesh
Than twenty times the value of the sum
That he did owe him; and I know, my lord,
If law, authority, and power deny not,
It will go hard with poor Antonio.

PORTIA
Is it your dear friend that is thus in trouble?

BASSANIO
The dearest friend to me, the kindest man,
293 The best-conditioned and unwearied spirit
In doing courtesies, and one in whom
The ancient Roman honor more appears
Than any that draws breath in Italy.

PORTIA
What sum owes he the Jew?

BASSANIO
For me, three thousand ducats.

PORTIA   What, no more?
299 Pay him six thousand, and deface the bond.
Double six thousand and then treble that,
Before a friend of this description
Shall lose a hair through Bassanio's fault.
First go with me to church and call me wife,
And then away to Venice to your friend!
For never shall you lie by Portia's side
With an unquiet soul. You shall have gold
To pay the petty debt twenty times over;
When it is paid, bring your true friend along.
My maid Nerissa and myself meantime
Will live as maids and widows. Come away!
311 For you shall hence upon your wedding day.
312 Bid your friends welcome, show a merry cheer;
Since you are dear bought, I will love you dear.

---

293 *best-conditioned* best natured   299 *deface* cancel   311 *hence* go hence
312 *cheer* countenance

But let me hear the letter of your friend.

[BASSANIO *(reads)*] 'Sweet Bassanio, my ships have all
miscarried, my creditors grow cruel, my estate is very
low, my bond to the Jew is forfeit. And since in paying
it, it is impossible I should live, all debts are cleared between you and I if I might but see you at my death.
Notwithstanding, use your pleasure. If your love do not
persuade you to come, let not my letter.'

PORTIA
O love, dispatch all business and be gone!

BASSANIO
Since I have your good leave to go away,
I will make haste, but till I come again
No bed shall e'er be guilty of my stay,
Nor rest be interposer 'twixt us twain.   *Exeunt.*

*

Enter [Shylock] the Jew and Solanio and Antonio   III, iii
and the Jailer.

SHYLOCK
Jailer, look to him. Tell not me of mercy.
This is the fool that lent out money gratis.
Jailer, look to him.

ANTONIO   Hear me yet, good Shylock.

SHYLOCK
I'll have my bond! Speak not against my bond!
I have sworn an oath that I will have my bond.
Thou call'dst me dog before thou hadst a cause,
But since I am a dog, beware my fangs.
The Duke shall grant me justice. I do wonder,
Thou naughty jailer, that thou art so fond   9
To come abroad with him at his request.

ANTONIO
I pray thee hear me speak.

III, iii A street in Venice   9 *naughty* wicked, corrupt; *fond* foolish

SHYLOCK

I'll have my bond. I will not hear thee speak.
I'll have my bond, and therefore speak no more.
I'll not be made a soft and dull-eyed fool,
To shake the head, relent, and sigh, and yield
To Christian intercessors. Follow not.
I'll have no speaking; I will have my bond.   *Exit.*

SOLANIO

It is the most impenetrable cur
19   That ever kept with men.   Let him alone;

ANTONIO

20   I'll follow him no more with bootless prayers.
He seeks my life. His reason well I know:
22   I oft delivered from his forfeitures
Many that have at times made moan to me.
Therefore he hates me.

SOLANIO   I am sure the Duke
Will never grant this forfeiture to hold.

ANTONIO

The Duke cannot deny the course of law;
27   For the commodity that strangers have
With us in Venice, if it be denied,
Will much impeach the justice of the state,
Since that the trade and profit of the city
Consisteth of all nations. Therefore go.
32   These griefs and losses have so bated me
That I shall hardly spare a pound of flesh
To-morrow to my bloody creditor.
Well, jailer, on. Pray God Bassanio come
To see me pay his debt, and then I care not!   *Exeunt.*

*

19 *kept* dwelt, associated   20 *bootless* fruitless   22 *delivered* saved   27
commodity trading rights or privileges; *strangers* non-Venetians, including
Jews   32 *bated* reduced

Enter Portia, Nerissa, Lorenzo, Jessica, and   III, iv
[Balthasar,] a Man of Portia's.

LORENZO

Madam, although I speak it in your presence,
You have a noble and a true conceit   2
Of godlike amity, which appears most strongly
In bearing thus the absence of your lord.
But if you knew to whom you show this honor,
How true a gentleman you send relief,
How dear a lover of my lord your husband,
I know you would be prouder of the work
Than customary bounty can enforce you.   9

PORTIA

I never did repent for doing good,
Nor shall not now ; for in companions
That do converse and waste the time together,   12
Whose souls do bear an equal yoke of love,
There must be needs a like proportion
Of lineaments, of manners, and of spirit ;
Which makes me think that this Antonio,
Being the bosom lover of my lord,
Must needs be like my lord. If it be so,
How little is the cost I have bestowed
In purchasing the semblance of my soul   20
From out the state of hellish cruelty !
This comes too near the praising of myself ;
Therefore no more of it. Hear other things :
Lorenzo, I commit into your hands
The husbandry and manage of my house   25
Until my lord's return. For mine own part,
I have toward heaven breathed a secret vow
To live in prayer and contemplation,
Only attended by Nerissa here,

III, iv Portia's house 2 *conceit* conception, attitude **9** *Than . . . you*
than ordinary kindness can make you **12** *waste* spend **20** *purchasing . . .
soul* i.e. redeeming Antonio, the likeness of Bassanio, 'my soul' **25**
husbandry care

Until her husband and my lord's return.
There is a monastery two miles off,
And there we will abide. I do desire you
33   Not to deny this imposition,
The which my love and some necessity
Now lays upon you.

LORENZO   Madam, with all my heart;
I shall obey you in all fair commands.

PORTIA
My people do already know my mind
And will acknowledge you and Jessica
In place of Lord Bassanio and myself.
So fare you well till we shall meet again.

LORENZO
Fair thoughts and happy hours attend on you!

JESSICA
I wish your ladyship all heart's content.

PORTIA
I thank you for your wish, and am well pleased
To wish it back on you. Fare you well, Jessica.

Exeunt [Jessica and Lorenzo].

Now, Balthasar,
As I have ever found thee honest-true,
So let me find thee still. Take this same letter,
And use thou all th' endeavor of a man
In speed to Padua. See thou render this
Into my cousin's hands, Doctor Bellario;
And look, what notes and garments he doth give thee
52   Bring them, I pray thee, with imagined speed
53   Unto the traject, to the common ferry
Which trades to Venice. Waste no time in words
But get thee gone. I shall be there before thee.

BALTHASAR
56   Madam, I go with all convenient speed.   *[Exit.]*

---

33 *imposition* duty, charge   **52** *imagined speed* swiftness of thought (?), all imaginable speed (?)   **53** *traject* (from Italian 'traghetto,' a ferry)   **56** *convenient* appropriate

PORTIA
 Come on, Nerissa; I have work in hand
 That you yet know not of. We'll see our husbands
 Before they think of us.
NERISSA   Shall they see us?
PORTIA
 They shall, Nerissa, but in such a habit   60
 That they shall think we are accomplishèd   61
 With that we lack. I'll hold thee any wager,
 When we are both accoutered like young men,
 I'll prove the prettier fellow of the two,
 And wear my dagger with the braver grace,
 And speak between the change of man and boy
 With a reed voice, and turn two mincing steps 67
 Into a manly stride, and speak of frays
 Like a fine bragging youth, and tell quaint lies, 69
 How honorable ladies sought my love,
 Which I denying, they fell sick and died –
 I could not do withal! Then I'll repent,   72
 And wish, for all that, that I had not killed them.
 And twenty of these puny lies I'll tell,
 That men shall swear I have discontinued school
 Above a twelvemonth. I have within my mind 76
 A thousand raw tricks of these bragging Jacks,
 Which I will practice.
NERISSA   Why, shall we turn to men? 78
PORTIA
 Fie, what a question 's that,
 If thou wert near a lewd interpreter!
 But come, I'll tell thee all my whole device
 When I am in my coach, which stays for us
 At the park gate; and therefore haste away,
 For we must measure twenty miles to-day. *Exeunt*.

*

60 *habit* costume 61 *accomplishèd* equipped 67 *reed* reedy, piping 69
quaint clever, contrived 72 *I . . . withal* I could not help it 76 *Above* more
than, i.e. at least 78 *turn to* turn into (with pun; cf. I, iii, 77)

III, v   *Enter [Launcelot the] Clown and Jessica.*

LAUNCELOT Yes truly; for look you, the sins of the father
are to be laid upon the children. Therefore, I promise you
3   I fear you. I was always plain with you, and so now I
4   speak my agitation of the matter. Therefore be o' good
cheer, for truly I think you are damned. There is but
one hope in it that can do you any good, and that is but a
7   kind of bastard hope neither.

JESSICA And what hope is that, I pray thee?

LAUNCELOT Marry, you may partly hope that your father
got you not – that you are not the Jew's daughter.

JESSICA That were a kind of bastard hope indeed! So the
sins of my mother should be visited upon me.

LAUNCELOT Truly then, I fear you are damned both by
father and mother. Thus when I shun Scylla your father,
15   I fall into Charybdis your mother. Well, you are gone
both ways.

JESSICA I shall be saved by my husband. He hath made
me a Christian.

LAUNCELOT Truly, the more to blame he! We were
20   Christians enow before, e'en as many as could well live
one by another. This making of Christians will raise the
price of hogs; if we grow all to be pork-eaters, we shall
23   not shortly have a rasher on the coals for money.

          Enter Lorenzo.

JESSICA I'll tell my husband, Launcelot, what you say.
Here he comes.

LORENZO I shall grow jealous of you shortly, Launcelot,
if you thus get my wife into corners.

JESSICA Nay, you need not fear us, Lorenzo. Launcelot
29   and I are out. He tells me flatly there's no mercy for me
in heaven because I am a Jew's daughter; and he says
you are no good member of the commonwealth, for in

III, v The same   3 *fear you* fear for you   4 *agitation* (blunder for 'cogita-
tion')   7 *neither* (simply emphasizes the statement)   15 *gone* done for
20 *enow before* i.e. numerous enough before Jessica became a Christian
23 *rasher* (of bacon)   29 *are out* have quarrelled

converting Jews to Christians you raise the price of
pork.

LORENZO *[to Launcelot]* I shall answer that better to the 33
commonwealth than you can the getting up of the
Negro's belly. The Moor is with child by you, Launcelot.

LAUNCELOT It is much that the Moor should be more 36
than reason; but if she be less than an honest woman, 37
she is indeed more than I took her for.

LORENZO How every fool can play upon the word!
I think the best grace of wit will shortly turn into 40
silence, and discourse grow commendable in none
only but parrots. Go in, sirrah; bid them prepare for
dinner

LAUNCELOT That is done, sir. They have all stomachs.

LORENZO Goodly Lord, what a wit-snapper are you!
Then bid them prepare dinner.

LAUNCELOT That is done too, sir. Only 'cover' is the 46
word.

LORENZO Will you cover then, sir?

LAUNCELOT Not so, sir, neither! I know my duty. 48

LORENZO Yet more quarrelling with occasion! Wilt thou 49
show the whole wealth of thy wit in an instant? I pray
thee understand a plain man in his plain meaning: go
to thy fellows, bid them cover the table, serve in the
meat, and we will come in to dinner.

LAUNCELOT For the table, sir, it shall be served in; for 54
the meat, sir, it shall be covered; for your coming in to 55
dinner, sir, why let it be as humors and conceits shall 56
govern.   *Exit Clown [Launcelot].*

---

33 *answer* justify   **36–37** *more than reason* larger than is reasonable (with
pun on *Moor*)   **37** *honest* chaste   **40** *best grace* highest quality   **46** *cover*
i.e. lay the table   **48** *Not so . . . duty* (to Launcelot *cover* now means to put on
his cap; cf. II, ix, 43)   **49** *quarrelling with occasion* i.e. quibbling   **54** *table*
(Launcelot quibbles with the word so that it now means the food itself)
55 *covered* served in a covered dish (?)   **56** *humors and conceits* whims and
ideas

LORENZO

58 O dear discretion, how his words are suited!
The fool hath planted in his memory
An army of good words; and I do know
61 A many fools that stand in better place,
62 Garnished like him, that for a tricksy word
63 Defy the matter. How cheer'st thou, Jessica?
And now, good sweet, say thy opinion –
How dost thou like the Lord Bassanio's wife?

JESSICA

Past all expressing. It is very meet
The Lord Bassanio live an upright life
For having such a blessing in his lady;
He finds the joys of heaven here on earth,
And if on earth he do not merit it,
In reason he should never come to heaven.
Why, if two gods should play some heavenly match
73 And on the wager lay two earthly women,
74 And Portia one, there must be something else
75 Pawned with the other, for the poor rude world
Hath not her fellow.

LORENZO   Even such a husband
Hast thou of me as she is for a wife.

JESSICA

Nay, but ask my opinion too of that!

LORENZO

I will anon. First let us go to dinner.

JESSICA

80 Nay, let me praise you while I have a stomach.

LORENZO

No, pray thee, let it serve for table-talk;

---

58 *dear discretion* precious discrimination; *suited* dressed up (?), used to suit the occasion (?)   61 *A many* many; *stand ... place* have higher social rank   62 *Garnished like him* i.e. resembling him   63 *Defy the matter* i.e. refuse to talk sense; *How cheer'st thou* what cheer   73 *lay* stake   74 *else* more   75 *Pawned* wagered   80 *stomach* inclination, appetite

Then howsome'er thou speak'st, 'mong other things   82
I shall digest it.

JESSICA   Well, I'll set you forth.   83

                              Exit [with Lorenzo].

                              *

              Enter the Duke, the Magnificoes, Antonio, Bassanio, IV, i
              [Salerio,] and Gratiano [with others].

DUKE What, is Antonio here?

ANTONIO Ready, so please your Grace.

DUKE
I am sorry for thee. Thou art come to answer
A stony adversary, an inhuman wretch,
Uncapable of pity, void and empty
From any dram of mercy.   6

ANTONIO   I have heard
Your Grace hath ta'en great pains to qualify   7
His rigorous course; but since he stands obdurate,
And that no lawful means can carry me
Out of his envy's reach, I do oppose
My patience to his fury, and am armed   11
To suffer with a quietness of spirit
The very tyranny and rage of his.

DUKE
Go one, and call the Jew into the court.

SALERIO
He is ready at the door; he comes, my lord.
              Enter Shylock.

DUKE
Make room, and let him stand before our face.   16
Shylock, the world thinks, and I think so too,

---

82 *howsome'er* however 83 *set you forth* serve you up, as at a feast; i.e.
praise you ironically
IV, i A Venetian court of justice 6 *From* of 7 *qualify* moderate 11
armed prepared 16 *our* my (the 'royal' plural)

18   That thou but leadest this fashion of thy malice
       To the last hour of act ; and then 'tis thought
20   Thou'lt show thy mercy and remorse more strange
       Than is thy strange apparent cruelty ;
       And where thou now exacts the penalty,
       Which is a pound of this poor merchant's flesh,
24   Thou wilt not only loose the forfeiture,
       But touched with human gentleness and love,
26   Forgive a moiety of the principal,
       Glancing an eye of pity on his losses,
       That have of late so huddled on his back –
29   Enow to press a royal merchant down
       And pluck commiseration of his state
       From brassy bosoms and rough hearts of flint,
       From stubborn Turks and Tartars never trained
33   To offices of tender courtesy.
       We all expect a gentle answer, Jew.

SHYLOCK

35   I have possessed your Grace of what I purpose,
       And by our holy Sabbath have I sworn
       To have the due and forfeit of my bond.
       If you deny it, let the danger light
39   Upon your charter and your city's freedom !
       You'll ask me why I rather choose to have
       A weight of carrion flesh than to receive
       Three thousand ducats. I'll not answer that,
       But say it is my humor. Is it answered ?
       What if my house be troubled with a rat,
       And I be pleased to give ten thousand ducats
46   To have it baned ? What, are you answered yet ?
47   Some men there are love not a gaping pig,
       Some that are mad if they behold a cat,

18–19 *thou . . . act* you but pursue this working of your malice to the last
minute **20** *remorse* pity **24** *loose* waive **26** *moiety* portion **29** *Enow*
enough; *royal merchant* (see III, ii, 239) **33** *offices* acts **35** *possessed*
informed **39** *freedom* (see III, ii, 278) **46** *baned* poisoned **47** *gaping pig*
i.e. served roasted with its mouth propped open

And others, when the bagpipe sings i' th' nose,
Cannot contain their urine; for affection,   50
Master of passion, sways it to the mood
Of what it likes or loathes. Now for your answer:
As there is no firm reason to be rend'red
Why he cannot abide a gaping pig,   54
Why he a harmless necessary cat,
Why he a woollen bagpipe, but of force   56
Must yield to such inevitable shame
As to offend, himself being offended;
So can I give no reason, nor I will not,
More than a lodged hate and a certain loathing   60
I bear Antonio, that I follow thus
A losing suit against him. Are you answered?   62

BASSANIO
This is no answer, thou unfeeling man,
To excuse the current of thy cruelty!

SHYLOCK
I am not bound to please thee with my answers.

BASSANIO
Do all men kill the things they do not love?

SHYLOCK
Hates any man the thing he would not kill?

BASSANIO
Every offense is not a hate at first.   68

SHYLOCK
What, wouldst thou have a serpent sting thee twice?

ANTONIO
I pray you think you question with the Jew.   70
You may as well go stand upon the beach
And bid the main flood bate his usual height;   72
You may as well use question with the wolf,

---

50 *affection* feeling, impulse   **54–56** *he . . . he . . . he* i.e. one man . . . another . . . a third   **56** *woollen bagpipe* (i.e. with flannel-covered bag); *of force* perforce   **60** *lodged* deep-seated   **62** *losing* unprofitable   **68** *offense* injury, grievance   **70** *think* keep in mind; *question* reason, argue   **72** *main flood* sea at flood tide; *bate* reduce

Why he hath made the ewe bleat for the lamb;
You may as well forbid the mountain pines
To wag their high tops and to make no noise
77 When they are fretten with the gusts of heaven;
You may as well do anything most hard
As seek to soften that – than which what's harder? –
His Jewish heart. Therefore I do beseech you
Make no moe offers, use no farther means,
82 But with all brief and plain conveniency
Let me have judgment, and the Jew his will.

BASSANIO
For thy three thousand ducats here is six.

SHYLOCK
If every ducat in six thousand ducats
Were in six parts, and every part a ducat,
87 I would not draw them. I would have my bond.

DUKE
How shalt thou hope for mercy, rend'ring none?

SHYLOCK
What judgment shall I dread, doing no wrong?
You have among you many a purchased slave,
Which like your asses and your dogs and mules
92 You use in abject and in slavish parts,
Because you bought them. Shall I say to you,
'Let them be free! marry them to your heirs!
Why sweat they under burdens? Let their beds
Be made as soft as yours, and let their palates
Be seasoned with such viands'? You will answer,
'The slaves are ours.' So do I answer you.
The pound of flesh which I demand of him
Is dearly bought, is mine, and I will have it.
If you deny me, fie upon your law!
There is no force in the decrees of Venice.
I stand for judgment. Answer; shall I have it?

77 *fretten* fretted 82 *conveniency* propriety 87 *draw* take 92 *parts* duties, functions

DUKE

Upon my power I may dismiss this court 104
Unless Bellario, a learned doctor
Whom I have sent for to determine this,
Come here to-day.

SALERIO   My lord, here stays without 107
A messenger with letters from the doctor,
New come from Padua.

DUKE

Bring us the letters. Call the messenger.

BASSANIO

Good cheer, Antonio! What, man, courage yet!
The Jew shall have my flesh, blood, bones, and all,
Ere thou shalt lose for me one drop of blood.

ANTONIO

I am a tainted wether of the flock, 114
Meetest for death. The weakest kind of fruit 115
Drops earliest to the ground, and so let me.
You cannot better be employed, Bassanio,
Than to live still, and write mine epitaph.
        Enter Nerissa [dressed like a Lawyer's Clerk].

DUKE

Came you from Padua, from Bellario?

NERISSA

From both, my lord. Bellario greets your Grace.
        [Presents a letter.]

BASSANIO

Why dost thou whet thy knife so earnestly?

SHYLOCK

To cut the forfeiture from that bankrout there.

GRATIANO

Not on thy sole, but on thy soul, harsh Jew,
Thou mak'st thy knife keen; but no metal can –
No, not the hangman's axe – bear half the keenness 125

104 *Upon* in accordance with 107 *stays without* waits outside 114
wether sheep 115 *Meetest for death* most fit for slaughter 125 *hangman's*
executioner's; *bear* have

Of thy sharp envy. Can no prayers pierce thee?

SHYLOCK

No, none that thou hast wit enough to make.

GRATIANO

128   O be thou damned, inexecrable dog,
129   And for thy life let justice be accused!
       Thou almost mak'st me waver in my faith –
131   To hold opinion with Pythagoras
       That souls of animals infuse themselves
       Into the trunks of men. Thy currish spirit
134   Governed a wolf who, hanged for human slaughter,
135   Even from the gallows did his fell soul fleet,
       And whilst thou layest in thy unhallowed dam,
       Infused itself in thee; for thy desires
       Are wolvish, bloody, starved, and ravenous.

SHYLOCK

Till thou canst rail the seal from off my bond,
Thou but offend'st thy lungs to speak so loud.
Repair thy wit, good youth, or it will fall
To cureless ruin. I stand here for law.

DUKE

This letter from Bellario doth commend
A young and learned doctor to our court.
Where is he?

NERISSA   He attendeth here hard by
To know your answer whether you'll admit him.

DUKE

With all my heart. Some three or four of you
Go give him courteous conduct to this place.
Meantime the court shall hear Bellario's letter.

150 [CLERK *(reads)*] 'Your Grace shall understand that at the

---

128 *inexecrable dog* dog that cannot be execrated enough   **129** *for thy life* i.e. because you are allowed to live   **131** *Pythagoras* Greek philosopher who believed in transmigration of souls   **134** *hanged* (animals were once hanged for 'crimes')   **135** *fell* cruel   **150** *Clerk* (no reader is designated in original texts, and it is possible that the letter is read by the Duke)

receipt of your letter I am very sick; but in the instant that
your messenger came, in loving visitation was with me a
young doctor of Rome. His name is Balthasar. I acquainted him with the cause in controversy between the Jew
and Antonio the merchant. We turned o'er many books
together. He is furnished with my opinion which, bet-
tered with his own learning, the greatness whereof I cannot enough commend, comes with him at my importunity   158
to fill up your Grace's request in my stead. I beseech you   159
let his lack of years be no impediment to let him lack a   160
reverend estimation, for I never knew so young a body
with so old a head. I leave him to your gracious accept-
ance, whose trial shall better publish his commendation.'   163
    *Enter Portia for Balthasar [dressed like a Doctor of
    Laws].*

DUKE
    You hear the learn'd Bellario, what he writes;
    And here, I take it, is the doctor come.
    Give me your hand. Come you from old Bellario?
PORTIA
    I did, my lord.
DUKE   You are welcome; take your place.
    Are you acquainted with the difference   169
    That holds this present question in the court?
PORTIA
    I am informèd throughly of the cause.   171
    Which is the merchant here? and which the Jew?
DUKE
    Antonio and old Shylock, both stand forth.
PORTIA
    Is your name Shylock?

---

158 *comes with him* i.e. he brings my opinion   159 *to fill . . . stead* in my place
in answer to your Grace's request   160 *to let him lack* i.e. which will cause
him to lack   163 *trial* i.e. actual performance   169–70 *with . . . court* i.e.
with the case being tried   171 *throughly* thoroughly; *cause* case

SHYLOCK   Shylock is my name.

PORTIA

    Of a strange nature is the suit you follow,

176   Yet in such rule that the Venetian law

    Cannot impugn you as you do proceed.

       [To Antonio]

178   You stand within his danger, do you not?

ANTONIO

    Ay, so he says.

PORTIA   Do you confess the bond?

ANTONIO

    I do.

PORTIA Then must the Jew be merciful.

SHYLOCK

    On what compulsion must I? Tell me that.

PORTIA

182   The quality of mercy is not strained;

    It droppeth as the gentle rain from heaven

    Upon the place beneath. It is twice blest;

    It blesseth him that gives and him that takes.

    'Tis mightiest in the mightiest; it becomes

    The thronèd monarch better than his crown.

    His sceptre shows the force of temporal power,

    The attribute to awe and majesty,

    Wherein doth sit the dread and fear of kings;

    But mercy is above this scept'red sway;

    It is enthronèd in the hearts of kings;

    It is an attribute to God himself,

    And earthly power doth then show likest God's

    When mercy seasons justice. Therefore, Jew,

    Though justice be thy plea, consider this:

197   That in the course of justice none of us

    Should see salvation. We do pray for mercy,

---

176 *in such rule* so within the rules   178 *danger* power, control   182 *strained* constrained, forced   197 *in . . . justice* i.e. if justice should actually run its course

And that same prayer doth teach us all to render
The deeds of mercy. I have spoke thus much
To mitigate the justice of thy plea,   201
Which if thou follow, this strict court of Venice
Must needs give sentence 'gainst the merchant there.

SHYLOCK
My deeds upon my head! I crave the law,
The penalty and forfeit of my bond.

PORTIA
Is he not able to discharge the money?

BASSANIO
Yes, here I tender it for him in the court,
Yea, thrice the sum. If that will not suffice,
I will be bound to pay it ten times o'er
On forfeit of my hands, my head, my heart.
If this will not suffice, it must appear
That malice bears down truth. And I beseech you,   212
Wrest once the law to your authority.   213
To do a great right, do a little wrong,
And curb this cruel devil of his will.

PORTIA
It must not be. There is no power in Venice
Can alter a decree establishèd.
'Twill be recorded for a precedent,
And many an error by the same example
Will rush into the state. It cannot be.

SHYLOCK
A Daniel come to judgment! yea, a Daniel!   221
O wise young judge, how I do honor thee!

PORTIA
I pray you let me look upon the bond.

SHYLOCK
Here 'tis, most reverend Doctor, here it is.

201 *justice . . . plea* your appeal to strict justice   212 *bears down* overwhelms
213 *Wrest . . . law* i.e. for once, subject the law   221 *Daniel* the shrewd
young man who exposed the elders in their false charges against Susannah

PORTIA
Shylock, there's thrice thy money off'red thee.

SHYLOCK
An oath, an oath! I have an oath in heaven;
Shall I lay perjury upon my soul?
No, not for Venice!

PORTIA   Why, this bond is forfeit;
And lawfully by this the Jew may claim
A pound of flesh, to be by him cut off
Nearest the merchant's heart. Be merciful.
Take thrice thy money; bid me tear the bond.

SHYLOCK
233   When it is paid, according to the tenor.
It doth appear you are a worthy judge;
You know the law, your exposition
Hath been most sound. I charge you by the law,
Whereof you are a well-deserving pillar,
Proceed to judgment. By my soul I swear
There is no power in the tongue of man
240   To alter me. I stay here on my bond.

ANTONIO
Most heartily I do beseech the court
To give the judgment.

PORTIA   Why then, thus it is:
You must prepare your bosom for his knife –

SHYLOCK
O noble judge! O excellent young man!

PORTIA
For the intent and purpose of the law
246   Hath full relation to the penalty,
Which here appeareth due upon the bond.

SHYLOCK
'Tis very true. O wise and upright judge!
How much more elder art thou than thy looks!

---

233 *tenor* substance of its terms   240 *stay* stand   246 *Hath full relation to* is completely in accord with

PORTIA
  Therefore lay bare your bosom.
SHYLOCK   Ay, his breast –
  So says the bond, doth it not, noble judge?
  'Nearest his heart'; those are the very words.
PORTIA
  It is so. Are there balance here to weigh   253
  The flesh?
SHYLOCK   I have them ready.
PORTIA
  Have by some surgeon, Shylock, on your charge,
  To stop his wounds, lest he do bleed to death.
SHYLOCK
  Is it so nominated in the bond?
PORTIA
  It is not so expressed, but what of that?
  'Twere good you do so much for charity.
SHYLOCK
  I cannot find it; 'tis not in the bond.   260
PORTIA
  You, merchant, have you anything to say?
ANTONIO
  But little. I am armed and well prepared.
  Give me your hand, Bassanio; fare you well.
  Grieve not that I am fall'n to this for you,
  For herein Fortune shows herself more kind
  Than is her custom: it is still her use
  To let the wretched man outlive his wealth
  To view with hollow eye and wrinkled brow
  An age of poverty; from which ling'ring penance
  Of such misery doth she cut me off.
  Commend me to your honorable wife.
  Tell her the process of Antonio's end,
  Say how I loved you, speak me fair in death;   273
  And when the tale is told, bid her be judge

253 *balance* scales   273 *speak me fair* speak well of me

275   Whether Bassanio had not once a love.
love ?   Repent but you that you shall lose your friend,
And he repents not that he pays your debt;
For if the Jew do cut but deep enough,
I'll pay it instantly with all my heart.

BASSANIO

Antonio, I am married to a wife
Which is as dear to me as life itself;
But life itself, my wife, and all the world
Are not with me esteemed above thy life.
I would lose all, ay sacrifice them all
Here to this devil, to deliver you.

PORTIA

Your wife would give you little thanks for that
If she were by to hear you make the offer.

GRATIANO

I have a wife who I protest I love.
I would she were in heaven, so she could
Entreat some power to change this currish Jew.

NERISSA

'Tis well you offer it behind her back;
The wish would make else an unquiet house.

SHYLOCK

These be the Christian husbands! I have a daughter;
294   Would any of the stock of Barabbas
Had been her husband, rather than a Christian!
We trifle time. I pray thee pursue sentence.

PORTIA

A pound of that same merchant's flesh is thine.
The court awards it, and the law doth give it –

SHYLOCK

Most rightful judge!

275 *love* friend's love **294** *Barabbas* a thief set free by Pontius Pilate when Christ was condemned; also the central character's name in Marlowe's *Jew of Malta*

PORTIA
 And you must cut this flesh from off his breast.
 The law allows it, and the court awards it.

SHYLOCK
 Most learnèd judge! A sentence! Come, prepare!

PORTIA
 Tarry a little; there is something else.
 This bond doth give thee here no jot of blood;
 The words expressly are 'a pound of flesh.'
 Take then thy bond, take thou thy pound of flesh;
 But in the cutting it if thou dost shed
 One drop of Christian blood, thy lands and goods
 Are by the laws of Venice confiscate
 Unto the state of Venice.   310

GRATIANO
 O upright judge! Mark, Jew. O learnèd judge!

SHYLOCK
 Is that the law?

PORTIA   Thyself shalt see the act;
 For, as thou urgest justice, be assured
 Thou shalt have justice more than thou desir'st.

GRATIANO
 O learnèd judge! Mark, Jew. A learnèd judge!

SHYLOCK
 I take this offer then. Pay the bond thrice
 And let the Christian go.

BASSANIO   Here is the money.

PORTIA
 Soft!
 The Jew shall have all justice. Soft, no haste;
 He shall have nothing but the penalty.

GRATIANO
 O Jew! an upright judge, a learnèd judge!

PORTIA
 Therefore prepare thee to cut off the flesh.
 Shed thou no blood, nor cut thou less nor more

But just a pound of flesh. If thou tak'st more
Or less than a just pound, be it but so much
326   As makes it light or heavy in the substance
Or the division of the twentieth part
328   Of one poor scruple – nay, if the scale do turn
329   But in the estimation of a hair –
Thou diest, and all thy goods are confiscate.

GRATIANO
A second Daniel! a Daniel, Jew!
332   Now, infidel, I have you on the hip!

PORTIA
Why doth the Jew pause? Take thy forfeiture.

SHYLOCK
Give me my principal, and let me go.

BASSANIO
I have it ready for thee; here it is.

PORTIA
He hath refused it in the open court.
He shall have merely justice and his bond.

GRATIANO
A Daniel still say I, a second Daniel!
I thank thee, Jew, for teaching me that word.

SHYLOCK
340   Shall I not have barely my principal?

PORTIA
Thou shalt have nothing but the forfeiture,
To be so taken at thy peril, Jew.

SHYLOCK
Why, then the devil give him good of it!
344   I'll stay no longer question.

PORTIA   Tarry, Jew!
The law hath yet another hold on you.
It is enacted in the laws of Venice,

326–27 *substance . . . division* quantity or a fraction   328 *scruple* a measure
of very light weight   329 *estimation of a hair* a hair's breadth   332 *on
the hip* (cf. I, iii, 42)   340 *barely* even   344 *stay . . . question* press my case
no further

If it be proved against an alien
That by direct or indirect attempts
He seek the life of any citizen,
The party 'gainst the which he doth contrive
Shall seize one half his goods; the other half
Comes to the privy coffer of the state;   352
And the offender's life lies in the mercy   353
Of the Duke only, 'gainst all other voice.
In which predicament I say thou stand'st,
For it appears by manifest proceeding
That indirectly, and directly too,
Thou hast contrived against the very life
Of the defendant, and thou hast incurred
The danger formerly by me rehearsed.   360
Down therefore, and beg mercy of the Duke.

GRATIANO

Beg that thou mayst have leave to hang thyself!
And yet, thy wealth being forfeit to the state,
Thou hast not left the value of a cord;
Therefore thou must be hanged at the state's charge.   365

DUKE

That thou shalt see the difference of our spirit,
I pardon thee thy life before thou ask it.
For half thy wealth, it is Antonio's;   368
The other half comes to the general state,
Which humbleness may drive unto a fine.   370

PORTIA

Ay, for the state, not for Antonio.

SHYLOCK

Nay, take my life and all! Pardon not that!
You take my house when you do take the prop
That doth sustain my house. You take my life
When you do take the means whereby I live.

---

352 *privy . . . state* personal funds of the sovereign **353** *lies in* lies at
360 *danger . . . rehearsed* penalty I have cited **365** *charge* expense **368**
For as for **370** *Which . . . fine* which humility on your part may reduce
to a fine

PORTIA
What mercy can you render him, Antonio?

GRATIANO
377   A halter gratis! Nothing else, for God's sake!

ANTONIO
So please my lord the Duke and all the court
379   To quit the fine for one half of his goods,
I am content; so he will let me have
The other half in use, to render it
Upon his death unto the gentleman
That lately stole his daughter.
Two things provided more: that for this favor
385   He presently become a Christian;
The other, that he do record a gift
Here in the court of all he dies possessed
Unto his son Lorenzo and his daughter.

DUKE
389   He shall do this, or else I do recant
The pardon that I late pronouncèd here.

PORTIA
391   Art thou contented, Jew? What dost thou say?

SHYLOCK
I am content.

PORTIA   Clerk, draw a deed of gift.

SHYLOCK
I pray you give me leave to go from hence.
I am not well. Send the deed after me,
And I will sign it.

DUKE   Get thee gone, but do it.

GRATIANO
In christ'ning shalt thou have two godfathers.
397   Had I been judge, thou shouldst have had ten more –
To bring thee to the gallows, not to the font.

Exit [Shylock].

377 *halter* hangman's noose   379 *quit* remit (?), substitute (?)   385
presently immediately   389 *recant* withdraw   391 *contented* i.e. willing to
accept these terms   397 *ten more* i.e. a jury of twelve

DUKE

Sir, I entreat you home with me to dinner.

PORTIA

I humbly do desire your Grace of pardon.
I must away this night toward Padua,
And it is meet I presently set forth.

DUKE

I am sorry that your leisure serves you not.   403
Antonio, gratify this gentleman,   404
For in my mind you are much bound to him.

Exit Duke and his Train.

BASSANIO

Most worthy gentleman, I and my friend
Have by your wisdom been this day acquitted
Of grievous penalties, in lieu whereof,   408
Three thousand ducats due unto the Jew
We freely cope your courteous pains withal.   410

ANTONIO

And stand indebted, over and above,
In love and service to you evermore.

PORTIA

He is well paid that is well satisfied,
And I delivering you am satisfied,
And therein do account myself well paid ;
My mind was never yet more mercenary.
I pray you know me when we meet again.
I wish you well, and so I take my leave.

BASSANIO

Dear sir, of force I must attempt you further.   419
Take some remembrance of us as a tribute,
Not as fee. Grant me two things, I pray you –
Not to deny me, and to pardon me.

PORTIA

You press me far, and therefore I will yield.

---

403 *your leisure . . . not* i.e. you do not have leisure   404 *gratify* reward
408 *in lieu whereof* in return for which   410 *cope* requite   419 *attempt you*
i.e. try to persuade you

Give me your gloves; I'll wear them for your sake.
[Bassanio takes off his gloves.]
And for your love I'll take this ring from you.
Do not draw back your hand; I'll take no more,
And you in love shall not deny me this.

BASSANIO

This ring, good sir, alas, it is a trifle!
I will not shame myself to give you this.

PORTIA

I will have nothing else but only this,
And now methinks I have a mind to it.

BASSANIO

432   There's more depends on this than on the value.
The dearest ring in Venice will I give you,
And find it out by proclamation.
435   Only for this, I pray you pardon me.

PORTIA

I see, sir, you are liberal in offers.
You taught me first to beg, and now methinks
You teach me how a beggar should be answered.

BASSANIO

Good sir, this ring was given me by my wife,
And when she put it on she made me vow
That I should neither sell nor give nor lose it.

PORTIA

That 'scuse serves many men to save their gifts.
And if your wife be not a madwoman,
And know how well I have deserved this ring,
She would not hold out enemy for ever
For giving it to me. Well, peace be with you!
Exeunt [Portia and Nerissa].

ANTONIO

My Lord Bassanio, let him have the ring.
Let his deservings, and my love withal,
Be valued 'gainst your wife's commandèment.

---

432 *more . . . value* more than the ring's value involved in this   **435** *for this*
as for this ring; *pardon me* i.e. release me from my obligation

BASSANIO

Go, Gratiano, run and overtake him;   450
Give him the ring and bring him if thou canst
Unto Antonio's house. Away, make haste!

Exit Gratiano.

Come, you and I will thither presently,
And in the morning early will we both
Fly toward Belmont. Come, Antonio.   *Exeunt.*

*

Enter [Portia and] Nerissa [disguised as before].   IV, ii

PORTIA

Inquire the Jew's house out, give him this deed,   1
And let him sign it. We'll away to-night
And be a day before our husbands home.
This deed will be well welcome to Lorenzo.

Enter Gratiano.

GRATIANO

Fair sir, you are well o'erta'en.   5
My Lord Bassanio upon more advice   6
Hath sent you here this ring, and doth entreat
Your company at dinner.

PORTIA   That cannot be.
His ring I do accept most thankfully,
And so I pray you tell him. Furthermore,
I pray you show my youth old Shylock's house.

GRATIANO

That will I do.

NERISSA   Sir, I would speak with you.
     [Aside to Portia]
I'll see if I can get my husband's ring,
Which I did make him swear to keep for ever.

PORTIA *[aside to Nerissa]*

Thou mayst, I warrant. We shall have old swearing   15

IV, ii A street in Venice 1 *deed* deed of gift 5 *o'erta'en* overtaken 6
advice consideration 15 *old* i.e. plenty of, continuous

That they did give the rings away to men;
But we'll outface them, and outswear them too. –
Away, make haste! Thou know'st where I will tarry.

NERISSA
Come, good sir, will you show me to this house?

[Exeunt.]

*

V, i   *Enter Lorenzo and Jessica.*

LORENZO
The moon shines bright. In such a night as this,
When the sweet wind did gently kiss the trees
And they did make no noise, in such a night
4   Troilus methinks mounted the Troyan walls,
And sighed his soul toward the Grecian tents
Where Cressid lay that night.

JESSICA   In such a night
7   Did Thisbe fearfully o'ertrip the dew,
8   And saw the lion's shadow ere himself,
And ran dismayed away.

LORENZO   In such a night
10   Stood Dido with a willow in her hand
11   Upon the wild sea banks, and waft her love
To come again to Carthage.

JESSICA   In such a night
13   Medea gathered the enchanted herbs
14   That did renew old Aeson.

LORENZO   In such a night
Did Jessica steal from the wealthy Jew,

V, i The park of Portia's house   **4** *Troilus* Trojan whose beloved but
false Cressida was sent away to the Greek camp   **7** *Thisbe* beloved of
Pyramus who fled from the lovers' meeting place when a lion approached
8 *ere* before   **10** *Dido* queen of Carthage loved and then deserted by
Aeneas; *willow* willow branch (symbol of forsaken love)   **11** *waft* beckoned
13 *Medea* enchantress in the legend of Jason and the Golden Fleece   **14**
Aeson Jason's father

And with an unthrift love did run from Venice   16
  As far as Belmont.
JESSICA   In such a night
  Did young Lorenzo swear he loved her well,
  Stealing her soul with many vows of faith,
  And ne'er a true one.
LORENZO   In such a night
  Did pretty Jessica, like a little shrow,   21
  Slander her love, and he forgave it her.
JESSICA
  I would out-night you, did nobody come;
  But hark, I hear the footing of a man.
      Enter [Stephano,] a Messenger.
LORENZO
  Who comes so fast in silence of the night?
MESSENGER A friend.
LORENZO
  A friend? What friend? Your name I pray you, friend.
MESSENGER
  Stephano is my name, and I bring word
  My mistress will before the break of day
  Be here at Belmont. She doth stray about
  By holy crosses where she kneels and prays   31
  For happy wedlock hours.
LORENZO   Who comes with her?
MESSENGER
  None but a holy hermit and her maid.
  I pray you, is my master yet returned?
LORENZO
  He is not, nor we have not heard from him.
  But we go in, I pray thee, Jessica,
  And ceremoniously let us prepare
  Some welcome for the mistress of the house.

16 *unthrift love* unthrifty love (?), unthrifty lover, i.e. Lorenzo (?)   21
shrow (form of the word 'shrew')   31 *holy crosses* wayside shrines marked
with crosses

Enter [Launcelot, the] Clown.

39 LAUNCELOT Sola, sola! wo ha! ho sola, sola!

LORENZO Who calls?

LAUNCELOT Sola! Did you see Master Lorenzo? Master
Lorenzo! sola, sola!

LORENZO Leave holloaing, man! Here.

LAUNCELOT Sola! where? where?

LORENZO Here!

LAUNCELOT Tell him there's a post come from my
master, with his horn full of good news. My master will
be here ere morning.   *[Exit.]*

LORENZO

Sweet soul, let's in, and there expect their coming.

And yet no matter; why should we go in?

51 My friend Stephano, signify, I pray you,

Within the house, your mistress is at hand,

And bring your music forth into the air. *[Exit Stephano.]*

How sweet the moonlight sleeps upon this bank!

Here will we sit and let the sounds of music

Creep in our ears; soft stillness and the night

57 Become the touches of sweet harmony.

Sit, Jessica. Look how the floor of heaven

59 Is thick inlaid with patens of bright gold.

There's not the smallest orb which thou behold'st

61 But in his motion like an angel sings,

62 Still quiring to the young-eyed cherubins;

Such harmony is in immortal souls,

64 But whilst this muddy vesture of decay

Doth grossly close it in, we cannot hear it.

[Enter Musicians.]

66 Come ho, and wake Diana with a hymn!

---

39 *Sola* imitation of a post horn (see ll. 46–47)   **51** *signify* announce   **57**
Become befit; *touches* notes, strains (with reference to fingering of an
instrument)   **59** *patens* metal plates or tiling   **61** *motion...sings* (reference
to the music of the spheres)   **62** *quiring* singing   **64** *muddy vesture* clay,
i.e. flesh   **66** *Diana* the moon goddess

With sweetest touches pierce your mistress' ear
And draw her home with music.
      Play music.

JESSICA

  I am never merry when I hear sweet music.

LORENZO

  The reason is, your spirits are attentive.
  For do but note a wild and wanton herd
  Or race of youthful and unhandled colts
  Fetching mad bounds, bellowing and neighing loud,
  Which is the hot condition of their blood:
  If they but hear perchance a trumpet sound,
  Or any air of music touch their ears,
  You shall perceive them make a mutual stand,   77
  Their savage eyes turned to a modest gaze
  By the sweet power of music. Therefore the poet
  Did feign that Orpheus drew trees, stones, and floods;   80
  Since naught so stockish, hard, and full of rage   81
  But music for the time doth change his nature.
  The man that hath no music in himself,
  Nor is not moved with concord of sweet sounds,
  Is fit for treasons, stratagems, and spoils;   85
  The motions of his spirit are dull as night,
  And his affections dark as Erebus.   87
  Let no such man be trusted. Mark the music.
      Enter Portia and Nerissa.

PORTIA

  That light we see is burning in my hall;
  How far that little candle throws his beams!
  So shines a good deed in a naughty world.   91

NERISSA

  When the moon shone we did not see the candle.

---

77 *make . . . stand* all stand still together   80 *feign* imagine; *Orpheus*
legendary musician; *drew* attracted, bent to his spell   81 *stockish* blockish,
dull   85 *spoils* plundering   87 *Erebus* classical place of darkness in the
region of hell   91 *naughty* wicked

PORTIA

So doth the greater glory dim the less.

94 A substitute shines brightly as a king
Until a king be by, and then his state
Empties itself, as doth an inland brook
Into the main of waters. Music! hark!

NERISSA

It is your music, madam, of the house.

PORTIA

99 Nothing is good, I see, without respect;
Methinks it sounds much sweeter than by day.

NERISSA

Silence bestows that virtue on it, madam.

PORTIA

The crow doth sing as sweetly as the lark
103 When neither is attended; and I think
The nightingale, if she should sing by day
When every goose is cackling, would be thought
No better a musician than the wren.

107 How many things by season seasoned are
To their right praise and true perfection!
Peace!

    [Music ceases.]

109   How the moon sleeps with Endymion,
And would not be awaked.

LORENZO   That is the voice,
Or I am much deceived, of Portia.

PORTIA

He knows me as the blind man knows the cuckoo –
By the bad voice.

LORENZO   Dear lady, welcome home.

PORTIA

We have been praying for our husbands' welfare,

---

94 *substitute* deputy (of the king)   **99** *without respect* without reference to
accompanying things; in itself   **103** *attended* with the other   **107–08** *by
season . . . perfection* i.e. are made perfect by coming at the right time
109 *Endymion* shepherd loved by the moon goddess

Which speed we hope the better for our words.
Are they returned?

LORENZO   Madam, they are not yet,
But there is come a messenger before
To signify their coming.

PORTIA   Go in, Nerissa.
Give order to my servants that they take
No note at all of our being absent hence –
Nor you, Lorenzo – Jessica, nor you.   121
    [A tucket sounds.]

LORENZO
Your husband is at hand; I hear his trumpet.
We are no telltales, madam; fear you not.

PORTIA
This night methinks is but the daylight sick;
It looks a little paler. 'Tis a day
Such as the day is when the sun is hid.
    Enter Bassanio, Antonio, Gratiano, and their
    Followers.

BASSANIO
We should hold day with the Antipodes   127
If you would walk in absence of the sun.

PORTIA
Let me give light, but let me not be light,   129
For a light wife doth make a heavy husband,   130
And never be Bassanio so for me.
But God sort all! You are welcome home, my lord.   132

BASSANIO
I thank you, madam. Give welcome to my friend.
This is the man, this is Antonio,
To whom I am so infinitely bound.

PORTIA
You should in all sense be much bound to him,
For, as I hear, he was much bound for you.

121 s.d. *tucket* short flourish of trumpets   127 *hold . . . Antipodes* i.e. share
daylight with the other side of the earth   129 *be light* i.e. be unfaithful
130 *heavy* sad   132 *sort* dispose

ANTONIO

138   No more than I am well acquitted of.

PORTIA

Sir, you are very welcome to our house.
It must appear in other ways than words;
141   Therefore I scant this breathing courtesy.

GRATIANO *[to Nerissa]*

By yonder moon I swear you do me wrong!
In faith, I gave it to the judge's clerk.
144   Would he were gelt that had it, for my part,
Since you do take it, love, so much at heart.

PORTIA

A quarrel ho! already! What's the matter?

GRATIANO

About a hoop of gold, a paltry ring
148   That she did give me, whose posy was
For all the world like cutler's poetry
Upon a knife – 'Love me, and leave me not.'

NERISSA

151   What talk you of the posy or the value?
You swore to me when I did give it you
That you would wear it till your hour of death,
And that it should lie with you in your grave.
155   Though not for me, yet for your vehement oaths,
156   You should have been respective and have kept it.
Gave it a judge's clerk! No, God's my judge,
The clerk will ne'er wear hair on's face that had it!

GRATIANO

He will, an if he live to be a man.

NERISSA

Ay, if a woman live to be a man.

GRATIANO

Now by this hand, I gave it to a youth,

138 *acquitted of* released from   141 *scant . . . courtesy* cut short this courtesy
of breath, i.e. of words   144 *gelt* gelded; *for my part* so far as I am concerned
148 *posy* inscription (commonly in verse)   151 *What* why   155 *Though . . .
yet for* even if not for my sake, still because of   156 *respective* careful

A kind of boy, a little scrubbèd boy   162
No higher than thyself, the judge's clerk,
A prating boy that begged it as a fee.
I could not for my heart deny it him.

PORTIA
You were to blame – I must be plain with you –
To part so slightly with your wife's first gift,
A thing stuck on with oaths upon your finger
And so riveted with faith unto your flesh.
I gave my love a ring, and made him swear
Never to part with it ; and here he stands.
I dare be sworn for him he would not leave it   172
Nor pluck it from his finger for the wealth
That the world masters. Now in faith, Gratiano,
You give your wife too unkind a cause of grief.
An 'twere to me, I should be mad at it.   176

BASSANIO *[aside]*
Why, I were best to cut my left hand off
And swear I lost the ring defending it.

GRATIANO
My Lord Bassanio gave his ring away
Unto the judge that begged it, and indeed
Deserved it too ; and then the boy, his clerk
That took some pains in writing, he begged mine ;
And neither man nor master would take aught
But the two rings.

PORTIA   What ring gave you, my lord ?
Not that, I hope, which you received of me.

BASSANIO
If I could add a lie unto a fault,   186
I would deny it ; but you see my finger
Hath not the ring upon it – it is gone.

PORTIA
Even so void is your false heart of truth.

162 *scrubbèd* scrubby, short   172 *leave* part with   176 *mad* distracted
186 *fault* misdeed

By heaven, I will ne'er come in your bed
Until I see the ring!

NERISSA   Nor I in yours
Till I again see mine!

BASSANIO   Sweet Portia,
If you did know to whom I gave the ring,
If you did know for whom I gave the ring,
And would conceive for what I gave the ring,
And how unwillingly I left the ring
When naught would be accepted but the ring,
You would abate the strength of your displeasure.

PORTIA

199   If you had known the virtue of the ring,
Or half her worthiness that gave the ring,
201   Or your own honor to contain the ring,
You would not then have parted with the ring.
What man is there so much unreasonable,
204   If you had pleased to have defended it
With any terms of zeal, wanted the modesty
206   To urge the thing held as a ceremony?
Nerissa teaches me what to believe;
208   I'll die for't but some woman had the ring!

BASSANIO

No, by my honor, madam! By my soul
210   No woman had it, but a civil doctor,
Which did refuse three thousand ducats of me
And begged the ring, the which I did deny him,
213   And suffered him to go displeased away—
Even he that had held up the very life
Of my dear friend. What should I say, sweet lady?
I was enforced to send it after him.
I was beset with shame and courtesy.

---

199 *virtue* power   201 *honor to contain* solemn duty to keep   204 *defended it* i.e. resisted giving it away   206 *urge* demand as a gift; *ceremony* token, keepsake   208 *but . . . had* if some woman didn't get   210 *civil doctor* doctor of civil law   213 *suffered* allowed

My honor would not let ingratitude
So much besmear it. Pardon me, good lady!
For by these blessèd candles of the night,
Had you been there I think you would have begged
The ring of me to give the worthy doctor.

PORTIA

Let not that doctor e'er come near my house.
Since he hath got the jewel that I loved,
And that which you did swear to keep for me.
I will become as liberal as you;
I'll not deny him anything I have,
No, not my body nor my husband's bed.
Know him I shall, I am well sure of it.
Lie not a night from home; watch me like Argus.   230
If you do not, if I be left alone—
Now by mine honor which is yet mine own,
I'll have that doctor for my bedfellow.

NERISSA

And I his clerk. Therefore be well advised   234
How you do leave me to mine own protection.

GRATIANO

Well, do you so. Let not me take him then!   236
For if I do, I'll mar the young clerk's pen.   237

ANTONIO

I am th' unhappy subject of these quarrels.

PORTIA

Sir, grieve not you; you are welcome notwithstanding.

BASSANIO

Portia, forgive me this enforcèd wrong,   240
And in the hearing of these many friends
I swear to thee, even by thine own fair eyes,
Wherein I see myself—

PORTIA   Mark you but that!
In both my eyes he doubly sees himself,

230 *Argus* mythological figure with a hundred eyes   234 *well advised* very
careful   236 *take* catch   237 *pen* i.e. penis   240 *enforcèd* unavoidable

In each eye one. Swear by your double self,
246 And there's an oath of credit.

BASSANIO   Nay, but hear me.
Pardon this fault, and by my soul I swear
I never more will break an oath with thee.

ANTONIO
I once did lend my body for his wealth,
Which but for him that had your husband's ring
Had quite miscarried. I dare be bound again,
My soul upon the forfeit, that your lord
253 Will never more break faith advisedly.

PORTIA
Then you shall be his surety. Give him this,
And bid him keep it better than the other.

ANTONIO
Here, Lord Bassanio. Swear to keep this ring.

BASSANIO
By heaven, it is the same I gave the doctor !

PORTIA
258 I had it of him. Pardon me, Bassanio,
For by this ring the doctor lay with me.

NERISSA
And pardon me, my gentle Gratiano,
For that same scrubbèd boy, the doctor's clerk,
262 In lieu of this last night did lie with me.

GRATIANO
Why, this is like the mending of highways
In summer, where the ways are fair enough.
265 What, are we cuckolds ere we have deserved it ?

PORTIA
266 Speak not so grossly. You are all amazed.
Here is a letter ; read it at your leisure.
It comes from Padua from Bellario.
There you shall find that Portia was the doctor,

---

246 *oath of credit* oath that can be believed (said ironically) 253 *advisedly*
intentionally 258 *of him* from him 262 *In lieu of* in return for 265
cuckolds deceived husbands 266 *amazed* lost in a maze, befuddled

Nerissa there her clerk. Lorenzo here
Shall witness I set forth as soon as you,
And even but now returned – I have not yet
Entered my house. Antonio, you are welcome,
And I have better news in store for you
Than you expect. Unseal this letter soon;
There you shall find three of your argosies
Are richly come to harbor suddenly.
You shall not know by what strange accident
I chancèd on this letter.

ANTONIO   I am dumb!

BASSANIO

Were you the doctor, and I knew you not?   *280*

GRATIANO

Were you the clerk that is to make me cuckold?

NERISSA

Ay, but the clerk that never means to do it,
Unless he live until he be a man.

BASSANIO

Sweet Doctor, you shall be my bedfellow.
When I am absent, then lie with my wife.

ANTONIO

Sweet lady, you have given me life and living!
For here I read for certain that my ships
Are safely come to road.   *288*

PORTIA   How now, Lorenzo?
My clerk hath some good comforts too for you.

NERISSA

Ay, and I'll give them him without a fee.
There do I give to you and Jessica
From the rich Jew, a special deed of gift,
After his death, of all he dies possessed of.

LORENZO

Fair ladies, you drop manna in the way
Of starvèd people.

288 *road* anchorage

PORTIA   It is almost morning,

296   And yet I am sure you are not satisfied
Of these events at full. Let us go in,

298   And charge us there upon inter'gatories,
And we will answer all things faithfully.

GRATIANO

Let it be so. The first inter'gatory
That my Nerissa shall be sworn on is,

302   Whether till the next night she had rather stay,
Or go to bed now, being two hours to day.
But were the day come, I should wish it dark

305   Till I were couching with the doctor's clerk.
Well, while I live I'll fear no other thing
So sore as keeping safe Nerissa's ring.   *Exeunt.*

296–97 *satisfied . . full* fully satisfied with the explanation of these events
298 *charge . . . inter'gatories* require ourselves there to answer interrogatories
(legally framed questions answerable under oath) **302** *stay* wait **305**
clerk (pronounced 'clark')

For a complete list of books available from Penguin in the United States, write to Dept. DG, Penguin Books, 299 Murray Hill Parkway, East Rutherford, New Jersey 07073.

For a complete list of books available from Penguin in Canada, write to Penguin Books Canada Limited, 2801 John Street, Markham, Ontario L3R 1B4.

If you live in the British Isles, write to Dept. EP, Penguin Books Ltd, Harmondsworth, Middlesex.